"KYLE, DON'T," SHE PLEADED WITH HER LAST OUNCE of resistance.

"Don't what?" he murmured, squeezing her waist gently.

"Don't . . . kiss me." Katherine licked her lips, knowing it was an invitation but unable to help herself, her mouth felt so dry. "I won't be able to resist you if you do."

"Why resist?"

That husky voice was going to undo her, and he hadn't even touched his sexy lips to hers yet. "It's not that simple. We're . . . different."

His thumb caressed her jaw, her neck, dipping low to touch the spot where her pulse tattooed a frantic beat. It was a struggle to continue to come up with reasons why he shouldn't kiss her when her eyes were crossed with lust. "We . . . don't like each other."

"I like you," he said, dipping his head so that his mouth hovered so tantalizingly close to her neck, she could feel his breath.

Her every muscle tensed in preparation for the feel of those lips. Her head even tilted a little, giving him access, but he didn't touch her. Not yet.

"I like you just fine," he whispered, and in the next instant, his mouth covered hers.

WHAT ARE *LOVESWEPT* ROMANCES?

They are stories of true romance and touching emotion. We believe those two very important ingredients are constants in our highly sensual and very believable stories in the LOVE-SWEPT line. Our goal is to give you, the reader, stories of consistently high quality that may sometimes make you laugh, sometimes make you cry, but are always fresh and creative and contain many delightful surprises within their pages.

Most romance fans read an enormous number of books. Those they truly love, they keep. Others may be traded with friends and soon forgotten. We hope that each LOVESWEPT romance will be a treasure—a "keeper." We will always try to publish

LOVE STORIES YOU'LL NEVER FORGET
BY AUTHORS YOU'LL ALWAYS REMEMBER

The Editors

Loveswept® 869

SHOW ME THE WAY

JILL
SHALVIS

BANTAM BOOKS

NEW YORK · TORONTO · LONDON · SYDNEY · AUCKLAND

SHOW ME THE WAY
A Bantam Book / January 1998

LOVESWEPT and the wave design are registered trademarks of
Bantam Books, a division of Bantam Doubleday Dell Publishing Group,
Inc. Registered in U.S. Patent and Trademark Office and elsewhere.

ISBN 0-553-44622-3

Published simultaneously in the United States and Canada

*Bantam Books are published by Bantam Books, a division of Bantam Dou-
bleday Dell Publishing Group, Inc. Its trademark, consisting of the words
"Bantam Books" and the portrayal of a rooster, is Registered in U.S. Patent
and Trademark Office and in other countries. Marca Registrada. Bantam
Books, 1540 Broadway, New York, New York 10036.*

PRINTED IN THE UNITED STATES OF AMERICA

OPM   10 9 8 7 6 5 4 3 2 1

I dedicate this one to Gary and Karyn. Without knowing it, you gave me the inspiration for this story. Thanks for the maps, the articles, the expertise. Thanks for last summer, and thanks most of all for Courtney!

PROLOGUE

Katherine Wilson was the cause of his ruination, and she would pay. With her life.

All he had to do now was get to her, which wasn't easy with the media making a circus of the courthouse.

The glory of that case she'd just tried should have been his alone, yet she'd stolen it. She'd become the darling of the media, and he hated that.

Not only had she stolen his life, she'd stolen his coverage.

He'd have killed her for that alone, but he had bigger fish to fry.

He wanted the senator's job, but if he wasn't careful, she'd climb the ranks and swipe it out from under him.

He wanted her dead. Oh, yeah. He wanted that, badly. But not until he'd destroyed her life as she'd destroyed his.

ONE

She absolutely couldn't believe what she was about to do. She was going camping, for God's sake. Katherine Wilson, successful prosecutor, was packing a *duffel bag*.

Katherine had to laugh at her reflection in her vanity mirror. Little makeup, hair scooped back in a ponytail, and jeans. *Jeans*. How long had it been since she'd had a free day off to dress as she pleased? If her office staff could see her now.

She sat on her bed and took a deep breath. She had to go within the hour. Her boss, Ted Houghton, district attorney, had insisted, and by now, she knew the arguments by heart.

It was true, she hadn't vacationed since . . . never. It was also true that her last case, the highly publicized drug trial of the senator's son, was over. She had the time off coming. But . . . camping? Relaxation didn't come easy for Katherine. Neither did enjoying idle time. She knew only hard work and dedication.

Unfortunately, neither would keep her safe now that

Richard Mohany, the senator's son, had been freed after his appeal had brought a hung jury. She hadn't expected to be in danger, but she'd come home from work to find Springer, her cocker-spaniel puppy, bludgeoned to death on her porch with a note that said she was next.

Mohany? Probably.

Ted had insisted on this immediate "vacation" to get her out of sight and out of mind, at least until the furor of the trial had died down.

Which was how she found herself driving four hours into the wilderness of the Sierras to go on a three-week guided camping trip courtesy of the DA's office. At the last minute she'd asked Ted if he felt it really necessary, hoping to get out of it. His answer had suitably frightened her.

"Go," he'd said, uncharacteristically grave on the phone. "You need to get out of the limelight for a little while. Did you get the equipment I sent?"

"Thanks." With her toe, she touched the framed backpack and the bag that had in it things she didn't want to think about—hiking boots, long underwear, a poncho, mittens, and a wool cap. "I don't think I'll need it all."

"Take it." In a gentler voice, he said, "You have to go, Katherine. It's the only way for now."

She tried not to think about her Springer. He'd been a gift, a frivolous addition that she had claimed not to want. But he'd grown on her alarmingly quickly in the few weeks she had him. She'd loved his huge brown eyes, the way he'd jumped and wiggled uncontrollably when she'd come home. . . . No. If she thought about him now, she'd break down. Katherine didn't, wouldn't, allow that.

"But if Mohany follows me, any others with me will be in danger—"

"He won't know where to find you. That's the beauty of this trip. Carry your beeper. I'll page you when it's safe."

"But—"

"No buts," Ted had said firmly, softening his voice. "It's the only way to keep you truly safe, Katherine."

She didn't need to add that what the man had done to Springer would haunt her forever, as did the thought of it happening to her. "But *camping*?"

He had actually chuckled. "A perfect revenge for the far-too-perfect Katherine Wilson. Try to enjoy yourself."

Enjoy herself? She'd forgotten the meaning, if she'd ever known it. "No," she'd said quickly. "I can't do it. I'll go into the Witness Protection Program. I can go work somewhere, anywhere, just for a little while."

"I dare you to do this," Ted had said softly, challenging her.

Damn him. "Fine. But I won't forget this."

During the entire drive to her designated meeting spot with her group, a state-park camping site in Kings Canyon National Park called Cedar Groves, Katherine fell into an old habit when things didn't go her way. She tried to find the pot of gold in the situation.

It wasn't to be found.

Ignoring the glorious mountain surroundings, the fresh air, the hum of nature, Katherine got out of her car. Fallen pine needles crunched beneath her feet. Little flutters of nerves plied her stomach. She told herself it was the severe altitude change from her ocean-level town of Sacramento to the nearly seven thousand feet she stood at now. It certainly couldn't be fear. She'd conquered that years before and rarely allowed herself to give in to such a weak emotion. Besides, Mohany would never find her. Not there.

She sighed. But no running water. No Chinese take-out. No steaming hot tea. What in the world had possessed her to agree to this?

The dare. Ted had dared her, and fool that she was, she'd yet to turn one down.

How childish it seemed now, with the warm, late-summer sun hitting her face, the breeze stirring her hair. There'd been other options. But she had to admit, the drastic change in temperature from the 105 degrees in the shade in her hometown to the 75 degrees where she stood now, was more than welcome. The woods around her seemed gigantic and deep. The mountains were so tall, she had to crane her neck to see the white-capped peaks. And the silence . . . there wasn't a sign of any movement.

In fact, she saw no sign of anyone. Her nerves knocked again, and she held her stomach as she popped two antacid tablets.

Vacation.

The very word inspired the shudders. She shouldn't be there. She had lots of work. Yeah, she'd take a lot of ribbing for backing out of such a simple thing, but what did she care? She was a grown-up. An attorney. She didn't have to jump at every dare as if she were back in high school. So Springer was gone. She'd deal with it. She'd just go into hiding for a couple of days, until Mohany either forgot about her or made another mistake. Easy.

Clutching her map in one hand and her tablets in the other, she whirled back to her car.

"Leaving already?"

Katherine hesitated, then slowly turned back.

A man—*a gorgeous man*—leaned negligently against a tree. His hair glinted like a buck's in the sun, lighting up with a gamut of sun-streaked browns and reds. His eyes were hidden behind reflective sunglasses. His body— long, lean, and rugged—looked as if it belonged there on the mountain.

"Here for Bonsai Trails?" he asked in a voice that went with his body; low and distinctly male.

Hadn't Ted mentioned Bonsai Trails was the name of the guiding company handling this trip? "Yes." It just occurred to her. Why did they need a guide? She could set up a tent. Or at least she thought she could. "But—"

"Ah, you're going to back out." His gaze seemed mocking, and knowing.

"I just—"

One corner of his mouth curved lazily. "Hey, it's all right. You don't have to apologize for chickening out. Lots of women do."

Her back straightened. *Backing out?* Katherine Wilson backed out of nothing. She raised her chin and gritted out, "I have no intention of 'chickening' out, whoever you are." He didn't have to know she'd been about to do that very thing.

"Kyle Spencer," he added helpfully, that infuriating smile firmly in place.

"Well, Mr. Spencer, as I was about to say, I just have to wait for . . ." For what? She had a hard time allowing herself to relax under the best of circumstances. With this man watching her, it would be impossible. His eyes, behind those glasses, seemed to miss nothing.

"For a good reason to hightail it out of here?"

Her hands actually clenched. Already, she needed another couple of tablets. And this was supposed to be vacation? "I told you, I'm not backing out." But oh, how she wanted to.

His smile grew. "Good. Name?" He consulted his clipboard.

"Katherine Wilson."

He nodded and checked her off. "The attorney. Saw you in the headlines recently. Explains the antacid," he added dryly.

She shoved them into her pocket. "You have a problem with attorneys?"

He grinned. "Not at the moment." He looked her up and down in a way that left her wondering if he could see right through her clothes. "Ever done this before, Katy?"

No one had called her that since childhood. "*Katherine.*"

He tilted his head. "You haven't, have you?"

"I've . . ." She stumbled over her words, struck by how very pathetic it would be to admit that, no, she'd never camped. She had never been given the chance to do something as frivolous as take time off, much less experiment with a tent. "Not exactly, no."

"Not exactly." He winced and let the clipboard fall to his side. "Great. Look, this isn't a trip for beginners. You should have realized that when you signed up."

"I didn't sign up," she mumbled, cursing both Mohany and Ted equally. "My boss is sending me on this trip."

"Well, he or she should have realized this is an intermediate trip, designed to increase strength and endurance."

"Strength—what does endurance have to do with camping?"

He groaned and shook his head. "Maybe you *should* quit."

"Why?" she demanded, suddenly determined not to.

"This isn't a little camping trip, Counselor. We won't be filing our nails at night while telling ghost stories over the campfire. We're going to be hiking ten miles a day. Then we'll raft down the white-water section of—"

"You're kidding."

"No," he said bluntly, shoving up his glasses, revealing a sharp pair of light brown eyes. "And I didn't even get to the part about the mountain biking over the rims of the canyons."

"Oh, God."

"Exactly."

She'd kill Ted when she saw him again. If she made it back alive. Just because she worked out faithfully on the StairMaster at the gym after work daily didn't mean she was prepared for this. But for some reason, she couldn't suppress a little glimmer of excitement. Hiking, rafting . . . biking.

"I'll get you a refund."

Suddenly he looked eager for her to back out. Well, she had a nasty surprise for him. "I'm not quitting, Mr. . . ." She smiled frostily, the same smile that had paralyzed hundreds of defendants on the stand. "I'm sorry, I forgot your name."

"Kyle Spencer." He sighed and pinched the bridge of

his nose. Without raising his head, he asked, in a resigned voice, "Are you in shape at all? Can you keep up?"

He didn't think she could. At that moment he couldn't have forced her to give up. A dare, after all, was a dare. "Of course."

"You're sure." He looked doubtful, but willing enough.

"I don't have a bike."

"It comes with the trip. We'll meet up with a sagwagon crew once a week for supplies."

Suddenly Katherine realized she was about to commit herself to a serious trekking expedition, not just a mere camping trip.

Did she really think she could handle this? It'd be easy to give in and back out. She could claim exhaustion from her job. After all, what did this man know about such things? He was a wanderlust sort of man, roaming the country at will, taking strangers along for the thrill of it. He probably hadn't made a sound commitment to serious work in his life. And he was so sure she couldn't do it.

Could she?

One look into Kyle's mocking eyes gave her the answer. "Are you in charge?"

Again, that cocky grin. "Yep."

"Know what you're doing?"

"You bet."

She knew he must. If nothing else, Ted wasn't negligent. He would have picked the best possible guide. Kyle's confidence, the very thing that irked her, also convinced her he'd more than do.

But he didn't look as sure. "We'll be a long way from

civilization, Counselor. No faxes, no computers, no phones."

For a minute fear bubbled up in her, mixing uneasily with the antacid. *No contact with the outside world.* Except the beeper in her back pocket.

What if Mohany found her after all?

Don't be silly, she told herself. How could he find her in the midst of the Sierras?

"If you want to give up in the middle," Kyle said, his eyes narrowed, "I'll have to say too bad."

Too bad. He had no idea how badly she wanted to run, not walk, back to her familiar surroundings. Bury herself back into her work without experiencing anything new. Anything that might shake her out of her safe, little cocoon.

But that cocoon *had* been shaken, shattered. And Springer was dead.

Live, a little voice inside her demanded. *Try it. You've never really tried it.* "I won't give up," she promised, swallowing her fear. She'd be safe enough, or at least as safe as she could get at the moment. "I'm going."

After a minute he shook his head. He slapped the clipboard against his jean-covered thigh. He took a deep breath, his shoulders stretching the material of his red Bonsai Trails T-shirt to the limit around well-developed biceps. Finally, he stuck out his hand, a very large, callused hand. "Very well. But I have a feeling you're in for a hell of a trip, Katy-the-attorney."

She bit her lip. Let's hope not, she thought. Let's hope not. But she took his large, warm hand with an outward calm—until they connected. The unfamiliar jolt shot up her elbow, down her body.

Startled, she looked up and met his suddenly intense gaze. Neither smiling nor frowning, he just held her hand and watched her, his powerfully built body absolutely still.

Finally, awkwardly, she pulled her hand away, but she felt the heat of his skin long after the connection between them was broken.

Kyle swore mildly to himself as he checked the packs one last time. What the hell was he supposed to do with a complete novice on a trip like he had planned? He should refuse to take her, but she had been stubborn and hardheaded about the entire thing, insisting she could handle herself.

"Just like an attorney," he muttered, risking a glance at the lady in question, who was sitting on a rock, serenely writing in a notebook.

Tall, willowy, and blond, she had the cool, perfect looks that would normally knock a man's socks off, legs so long and toned, they should have been illegal. He was immune to such things, or so he told himself. But those gray eyes . . . they hadn't been cool at all, but warm and sultry, and full of secrets. Haunting secrets.

When he'd touched her he'd felt her start of surprise, and knew exactly what had caused it. Something had . . . happened between them.

He grimaced. *Great.* To be fantasizing about a client . . . He must have been out on the trail too long. Nearly all summer already. Soon his season would be over and Bonsai Trails would close up again until next summer. The thought only saddened him, because he knew what was waiting for him back home—his position as vice-president in charge of research and development for GO!, otherwise known as Spencer's Great Outdoors.

The internationally famed outdoor-equipment company was his great-grandfather's legacy, and there had been a Spencer running the worldwide corporation for nearly a hundred years. As the oldest and only son, Kyle had a lead position and was being primed for the day his father retired.

Kyle loved it, he really did. But he loved the real outdoors more, *much more*. And in return for his commitment to the family business, the company gave him his two months off every year to run Bonsai Trails.

The great outdoors. He lived for it, craved it, felt at one with it. And knowing that he still had one more trip after this before it was over for another year allowed him to relax.

He wouldn't let anything ruin it. Certainly not one beautiful, if incredibly obstinate, attorney. Smiling as he stood, he thought there might be some justice after all. Katy swatted irritatedly at a fly, then nearly lost her balance on the rock. His grin grew. Yep, it just might be fun to watch the formidable Katherine Wilson fight her way through the woods instead of through a trial.

She had no idea what she was in for.

"Okay, we're ready," Kyle called to the eclectic group of five travelers sitting around. It was, for him, a relatively small group, made up of a couple from L.A., a brother-and-sister duo from Oregon, and Katy. He gave them his usual pep talk, telling them how much fun they were in for, what an adventure they were going to have. His own adrenaline kicked in, as it always did at the start of a new trip.

"You should have all read the guidebook Bonsai Trails sent you." He sent a long-suffering look to Katy, who had obviously not gotten hers from whoever had set her up for the trip. "But for those of you who are unprepared, here it is."

He ignored her narrowed look. "First of all, this is a vacation. So leave the phones, the mini-faxes, and the beepers in your cars. You won't be needing them."

"Thank God," someone muttered, and Kyle couldn't agree more. He'd have plenty of that life when he closed up Bonsai Trails for the season and returned to the city.

"We'll be tooling through the deep glacial canyons of Kings Canyon National Park," he said. "And let me tell you, folks, the beauty you'll see will rival anything you'll ever lay your eyes on. We're going through the South Fork Canyon, a true wilderness." Out of the corner of his eye, he saw Katherine shift uncomfortably and, out of sheer perversity, decided to increase that discomfort. "It's secluded, hardly ever visited, probably one of the most remote regions of the United States. For five days we're on our own there, with a brief respite on day four. I've divvied up our supplies amongst all our packs. On the sixth day we'll meet up with the sag wagon and get our rafts and more supplies." He managed to look serious. "So don't lose anything, especially the food. I get real hungry by the end of the day."

Everyone laughed but Katy. *Figured.* She was long on legs, short on sense of humor. He'd found most beautiful women were. "Then we'll have another day off before starting down the river. After another five days we'll meet up with more supplies and our bikes."

There were smiles of approval this time—and anticipation. From everyone, that was, except the counselor. "Rule one," he continued with a little smile. "Stay with me. Stay beside me, behind me, I don't care. *Just stick with me.* Leave no signs you've been here. Also pick up every little scrap of trash. And don't, *please*, wander off on your own unless you've cleared it with me, especially at night after we've camped."

He sensed Katy the attorney's disapproval. Or fear. Her light brows knit together tightly and her red lips pursed. Would she wear lipstick on the entire trek? As long as she managed to carry her own gear and her portion of the food and supplies, he shouldn't have cared. "Got a problem, Katy?"

"Katherine," she grated, giving him some satisfaction. He actually had no idea why he baited her, but it was fun watching those stormy eyes flare as she struggled for the control that obviously meant so much to her. "Is this trip . . . dangerous?"

He bit back his grin, knowing by the look in those eyes exactly how much it had cost her considerable pride to ask. "Only if you're stupid. But if you'd like to back out . . ."

"No." She took a deep breath, as though struggling for calm. "Just asking."

"It's not necessarily dangerous," he relented in a kinder voice. "Not if you listen carefully and pay attention." He glanced at the others. "There are bears. There are snakes, mostly *not* poisonous. Some of the bike trails are narrow, with steep falls if you're not watching. And the river can be fast and tricky. It's all in how you play this, ladies and gentleman. And I plan to play it very safe, believe me." He glanced at his novice again. She flushed.

Knowing he'd suitably scared her, he didn't dare give in to his urge to laugh. Hopefully, she'd swallow some of that swollen ego and actually listen. But he had a feeling Katherine Wilson didn't often let go of her tightly held control, and then trust someone else to keep it for her. She seemed to define the word *stubborn*.

But Kyle could be just as stubborn when the mood struck him, as it had the moment he'd set eyes on her. *He* was in control here, in his element. Just as she was miles from hers. She was about to learn how to let someone else be in charge, the hard way. Even if she had eyes that unaccountably drew him and a body that mesmerized him.

"Well, suit up, everyone. It's show time."

TWO

Disappearing into the mountains wouldn't save Katherine Wilson, he thought viciously. Not by a long shot, not after what she'd done to him.

She might think she could escape without harm, but he wouldn't let her do it again. Couldn't let her do it again. Not when the stakes were so very high.

Yet his favorite game had always been cat and mouse.

Maybe he'd let her run as far as she could, then slowly hunt her down. Yeah, that might be fun. Then he could play and torment her awhile, watch the fear and anxiety grow in her eyes as she realized how helpless she really was.

After all, he'd thoroughly enjoyed scaring her over what he'd done to her damn puppy. More of that would be a pleasure.

Toying with the formidable Katherine Wilson.

Hmmmmm. That sounded like fun indeed.

Less than an hour into the hike, Katherine seriously had to doubt her sanity. Her legs ached, her lungs screamed. She'd broken three nails.

And she was petrified.

She drew a ragged breath and reached for the water bottle strapped to her hip. Despite the relatively cool day, sweat ran down her temples, down her spine, and pooled uncomfortably at the base of her back. Insects buzzed around her while the slight wind rustled the foliage. It wasn't necessarily the walk overheating her system.

Each little thing, every little sight and smell, slammed home the realization of how isolated she was. No phone. No radio. No help. Miles and miles of tall canyons, huge, towering trees, and deep river gorges . . . and Mohany could be hiding anywhere. Behind any tree, beyond any rock. Visions of Springer's broken and bloody body danced in her head. The wild outdoors suddenly became just that—wild and uncontrollable.

Why had she agreed to this?

Kyle had been right. This hike was relentless, if incredibly beautiful. He moved surefooted in front of her, showing no signs of slowing down. When he turned, he gave her a little smile. "Not tired yet, are you?"

His smile was surprisingly free of sarcasm or smirk, but still it got her goat. "Nope." With the ease of a great actor—or an attorney—she smiled back just as sweetly, which faded the instant he turned back around. She inwardly groaned and chugged down gulps of deliciously cool water.

Bottom line—she thought she just might die.

"Ugh! This . . . is harder than it was . . . last year."

Katherine glanced over her shoulder at the petite red-head hiking behind her, also huffing tremendously. Her name was Sarah, and her brother, Jonathan, walking behind her, laughed.

"I told you that extra five pounds would get you. Plus you're getting old."

"Shut . . . up." But even that was uttered without rancor. "I'm only twenty . . . two," she panted. "Young enough to still kick your butt if I need to."

Jonathan laughed again. His long red hair stuck to his head, matted down by sweat. "Try it, baby. Just try it. But as your twin, I don't advise it."

The trail was narrow as it wound its way up to the top of the ridge. Swaying pines provided soothing shade, and heavy growths of brush kept the ground cool. Still, Katherine felt unbearably hot—and shaken over what she'd agreed to do for the next few weeks. But one glance at Kyle's back told her what she already knew. She wouldn't quit.

She couldn't see the couple she knew walked behind Sarah and Jonathan, and she could hardly muster up the energy to talk, but she had her insatiable curiosity to deal with. Besides, she'd already meticulously planned out Ted's slow and torturous death, and if she stopped keeping her mind busy, she'd dwell on things best left alone.

"You've done this before?" she asked Sarah, using the conversation as a tactic to slow down. Her body greedily sucked in oxygen.

"Yeah." Sarah swiped at her forehead and readjusted her pack. "Crazy, huh?"

Definitely. Katherine wasn't sure why anyone would do this more than once to themselves.

"Save your breath, ladies," Kyle shot over his shoulder with what could only be described as a wicked grin. "We're going to crest this peak today, even go beyond it. You'll need your energy. I'm not carrying any of you, especially you, Legs." He raised his eyebrows at Katherine before turning back around.

Legs? No man got away with that. If someone in her office had dared, she would have shot him down with just a look. She would have told Kyle so, too, if she had had the breath.

"Last one up does dishes!" he called back.

Katherine glanced at Kyle's sturdy back, his wide shoulders easily carrying his heavy load, which far outweighed any of theirs. His long legs churned up the path with little to no effort. He hadn't broken a sweat.

She hated him.

"God, he's in great condition." This came from Bettina, the wife of Chris. They caught up easily with Sarah and Jonathan, then passed Katherine with a sympathetic smile.

"Hurry up, babe," Chris said, lightly swatting his wife's shapely behind. "I'm not doing dishes."

"Oh, don't worry," Kyle quipped over his shoulder, "the counselor is."

Katherine burned. If only she could catch up with him, she'd . . . probably collapse at his feet in a pathetic, whimpering mass of jelly. "Let me get this straight," she huffed to Sarah. "You've done this before. With *him*?"

"Yeah."

"And you're paying money to do it *again*?"

"Yeah. Isn't he great?" Sarah whispered back with a conspiratorial grin.

Jonathan rolled his eyes at his sister, then looked at Katherine. "This is our fifth Bonsai Trails trek. Kyle runs it. He's taken us three times now, and he's the best guide there is, no comparison."

Katherine closed her mouth, sure that the jury was still out on that one. But she trudged along, proud of herself for forgetting her fear. If only for a minute.

Suddenly the ground shuddered violently beneath her feet and a loud crash reverberated through the woods around them.

Katherine froze, panicked. *He'd found her, and he'd brought a gun!*

"Wow," Sarah whispered in front of her, sounding awed. "Did you see that, Jonathan?"

"Yeah." In the back of her dimmed, numbed mind, Katherine was aware of Jonathan stopping and shaking his head. "I've always wondered," he breathed.

"Me too." Kyle came back toward them, an easy smile on his face. "Well, gang, now you know the truth to the eternal question. A tree falling in the woods *does* make a sound. A hell of one."

A falling tree. That's all it was. Not the senator's son with his twisted need for revenge, positive he could beat the system because he'd always done so in the past.

"As you can see," Kyle continued, lifting a long, tanned arm and pointing out into the steep drop-off to their right. "California's long drought really took its toll. A quarter of those trees out there are dead. They'll fall, too, eventually."

A falling tree, Katherine repeated slowly to herself,

lifting a hand to her pounding heart. She would have laughed at herself, if she could. But her heart had lodged in her throat. Her limbs were stiff. Or she'd thought they were, but that was before she found herself sinking to the ground on rubbery legs.

"Katy?" Kyle frowned and dropped to his knees before her, taking her hands in his. They were ice-cold. "What's the matter?"

She laughed, a slightly hysterical sound that had him frowning deeper. Kyle didn't picture the counselor easily spooked, but something had done just that. Her face had gone ashen, but now she had two spots of color on her cheeks.

"It was just a tree falling," she said inanely.

"Yes. Just a tree." He narrowed his eyes as she ripped her hands from his and tried to stand. "Wait a minute. Dammit, I said wait," he said quickly as she wavered again. He held her shoulders until she stilled, then slipped off her backpack. He was surprised at how fragile she felt, how slender, and he kicked himself for not keeping the pace easier. Or for not making her stay home. "Jonathan, get me some water, could you, please?"

"I don't need any water," Katherine insisted, pushing his hands away and giving him an indignant stare. "I didn't faint, you know."

The color returned to her face, which relieved him. So did the show of temper, since it meant she was on the mend. Sitting back on his heels, he studied her carefully. "What happened, then?"

"Nothing." She stood and took a few steps away from everyone who had crowded around her, concerned. "Better hurry," she said in a casual voice that didn't fool him, since he saw her hand tremble slightly as she hitched her pack back on. "Or you'll end up doing dishes."

He let her go after a few minutes, after insisting she stop again so he could lighten up her pack a bit, but he kept close behind her on the remote dirt track that wound its way along, trapped between a mountain two thousand feet up on the left and a twelve-hundred-foot drop on the right. The day was a stunner; a brilliant blue sky without a cloud in sight. The green of the forest surrounded them, so did the scents of pine and the hum of the live mountain. There were no more falling trees.

Just what the hell had she thought happened back there? An earthquake? No, not enough of an earth movement. He had to admit, she had him stumped. But he'd get to the bottom of her palpable fear, he promised himself. He couldn't have her jumping at every little noise or she'd be a wreck before they even got on the rafts.

Kyle watched her set her shoulders squarely and raise her chin. *Bravado*, he thought. *Just bravado*. He knew he shouldn't have let her come, but there was something about her . . . something that had told him she needed this trip as badly as he did.

"On vacation?" he asked conversationally when he'd caught up with her.

She kept her gaze straight ahead. "Yes."

Her voice was curt. A definite, don't-bother-me-with-banal-conversation voice, which didn't deter him in the least. "I'm surprised you managed to leave your beeper and mobile phone at home."

She blinked, but still didn't look at him.

"So, do you get people out of trouble or lock them away?"

"Lock them away."

A prosecutor. That only slightly redeemed her profession in his eyes. The breeze blew at her ponytail. Her long legs moved gracefully. "Sounds like a cushy job," he ventured, knowing this would only rile her again. But temper kept her moving.

She laughed, a light breathless sound. Then she shoved at her bangs, exposing incredibly gray eyes. "That's funny, coming from you."

"Why?"

"What would you know about hard work?"

He actually tripped then, over his own damn boots no less. Thankful that the rest of the group were at least twenty yards back on the trail, he struggled between the urge to strangle her and to defend himself. Well aware that most people assumed he took ten months off after he'd closed Bonsai Trails for the year, and that they didn't view his lifestyle as particularly difficult, he had long ago gotten used to the fact that a sort of playboy reputation followed him around.

But for some reason, he'd expected more from the counselor. "This isn't hard enough for you?"

"You know what I meant."

"What would you say," he asked casually, "if I told you I run a multimillion-dollar corporation?"

She laughed. He burned.

"Why," he asked in a surprisingly even voice, "is that so hard to believe?" If her smile hadn't been so damned sexy, he might have gritted his teeth.

"You're not the business type."

She looked so sure, and now he did grit his teeth. "And what, exactly, is the business type?"

Running her tongue over her teeth, she looked him over. For the first time he felt underdressed in his favorite clothes.

"The business type," she told him with a slightly patronizing smile that made him want to both strangle and kiss her, "is a man who's more comfortable with a computer than a mountain."

"I can work a computer." Actually, he was an expert, but he was far more proud of his survival skills.

Again her gaze ran over him. "I can't picture you behind a desk, running a business."

That's because he rarely sat behind his desk but used his laptop. "Because I wear jeans?"

"Because you camp for a living."

Three squirrels scattered from the path. Normally, that would have thrilled him, but this woman had him in knots without trying. "If you're so disdainful of what I do, why did you come?"

She didn't answer. Right then he should have told her the truth about himself, but he didn't. If she didn't like him for being himself and doing what he loved, then he'd forget her.

More easily said than done.

The path narrowed. He let her take the lead, and even as annoyed as he was, he enjoyed watching her move as much as he enjoyed the surroundings.

When she stumbled slightly ahead of him, her boot catching on a low root, he called out for a lunch break, not missing her brief glance of gratitude. He told himself he'd called the break because his other clients needed one, and for no other reason.

But God, she looked sweet as she allowed her shoulders to sag with growing exhaustion. Holding back his smile, he said casually, "Unless, of course, you're not ready to stop. We could go another mile or two if you insist."

"No!" she said quickly, dropping her pack. "I don't want to push anyone . . . especially if you're hungry."

She sank to a fallen stump, not quite hiding her sigh of relief. The others dropped their packs as well. Sarah plopped down next to her and groaned loudly.

"Good Lord, I'm out of shape this time, Kyle. How much further today?".

"Is everyone beat?" he asked, looking around. Jonathan and Chris looked fine. So did Bettina. Only Sarah and Katherine looked the worse for wear. But he knew Sarah could do it. "Can we get to the next ridge today? It's three more miles."

Sarah lay back on her elbows, tipping her head up to see the top of the crest. "I can do it." She looked at Katy. "Think you can?"

Katherine's eyes met with Kyle's for one brief, telling instant. They went hard with determination. "If you can, I can."

He couldn't help it. Despite the fact she annoyed the hell out of him, despite the fact she didn't respect what he did, and vice versa, and that she would slow them all down over the next three weeks, in that moment he admired her greatly.

That is, until she smiled her lethal smile and said, "Kyle, you're the last to step over here. Looks like you're doing dishes tonight."

Katherine dropped her pack and pretended nonchalance at the victory of ten miles straight up in one day. That is, until everyone had separated a little, and she found herself alone.

Then she collapsed to the hard ground and tried not to remember her lovely, soft bed at home, tried not to whimper pathetically at her various aches and pains, tried not to think about how good a long, hot shower would feel. . . .

"Isn't this terrific?" Sarah asked gleefully, sinking to the ground next to Katherine. Flipping back her long red hair, she leaned on her elbows and studied the incredible view around them. Tall pines surrounded them on what looked to be a sort of rock plateau. Below lay a green, lush valley. "There's no place I'd rather be."

Katherine could think of several; top on the list—a five-star restaurant. "Hmm."

"You don't sound like you agree."

"I'm not really very good at this outdoor thing," Katherine admitted, stretching out her screaming legs. Her poor toes, which hadn't been in anything other than expensive leather pumps until today, hurt so badly, she was afraid to take off her boots, knowing she'd never get them back on. Something creepy-crawly, with far too many legs, crossed her vision, and she sat up hastily, watching warily as the icky thing moved out of sight under a rock.

A deep, husky laugh sounded behind her. "Keep jumping like that every time you see a bug, Legs, and you'll be leaping your way through the South Fork Canyon."

Okay, this wasn't going to work out for her, she decided. Kyle's tall, rangy body moved closer, then he easily squatted before them. Her eyes were immediately drawn to his tight thighs, wondering how in the world they could possibly be holding him up with such ease after what they'd climbed. But those taut muscles looked as if they could handle anything.

No. She wasn't—yes, she was. Oh, God. She was *lusting*. Nope, this wasn't going to work out, not at all. She wondered if she could make it the ten miles back to her car, and had started to rise to her feet when she gasped in pain.

"What's the matter?" Kyle asked immediately, reaching for her.

"Nothing," she managed to say quite normally. She'd die before admitting her feet hurt. "Go away."

He put his hands on her shoulders and firmly sat her back down. Before she could budge, he'd pulled her feet toward him and had the new boots unlaced. Carefully, he eased one off, then swore with amazing vulgarity. "You're only wearing one pair of socks."

"So?"

He groaned, then peeled the sock back while she sat straight up in embarrassment. "Hey!" she protested, trying to pull back, but he held her ankle in a steel grip.

"Hold still," he commanded, frowning, his attention completely on her foot. His long, tanned fingers ran over her skin, causing her to yelp. "My fault," he said grimly, shaking his head.

"What?" Now her voice came shockingly unsteady, and it had little to do with the pain he was causing her. In fact, she could hardly feel it. Not when she was all too aware of his fingers running over her skin. She tingled, she burned, and it annoyed the hell out of her. How could a touch on the foot seem so intimate, so unbearably erotic?

"I knew you were a novice," he said with disgust aimed entirely at himself. "Sarah, could you get me my pack?" While he waited he removed her other boot, and no matter how she protested, he ignored her. "You're blistered pretty good, Katy. But I'll fix you up."

"Dr. Kyle?" she asked, wincing at how breathless she sounded.

At the sound of her voice, his head snapped up and his gaze searched hers. "Maybe." Those fingers squeezed and caressed while his eyes held hers. Whatever he found there, in her expression, caused his eyes to flare with heat, and the breath backed up in her throat.

"Here, Kyle," Sarah said, crunching through the foliage back to where they sat. "Don't worry, Katherine. Kyle is fantastic with blisters. You'll be fine tomorrow."

But Katherine's eyes had narrowed on the needle in Kyle's hand and how he quickly sterilized it with a match. All lingering sense of hazy sensuality fled. "What," she asked quickly, "are you planning on doing with that?"

Again, his gaze met hers, this time with sympathy. "It won't hurt any more than it already must."

"No."

"If you hold your foot real still," he said, setting her foot in his lap and reaching for one of her hands with his free one, "I'll hold your hand while I do it."

The cajoling, coaxing tone his deep, husky voice had taken on could seduce a nun. But not Katherine. She was no stranger to men and their ways, and she wasn't having it. "No." She yanked back her hand.

"Okay," he said easily, still holding her captive with his soft, light brown eyes. "Wow, look at that. It's getting dark already. Isn't that a gorgeous sunset? Sarah?"

"Gosh, it is," she gushed so sweetly that Katherine followed their line of vision and watched the glorious sun as it began its descent beyond the closest peak.

The sky around the brilliant sun burst with oranges and reds, mixed into a swirl of blues and deep purples. A gentle breeze blew over Katherine's face, cooling her. Far above, the pines and sequoias swayed. So lovely, so peaceful. Except for one Kyle Spencer, who inspired anything but peaceful, lovely feelings in her.

Katherine had never met a man who hadn't been completely blown over by her looks, by her accomplishments. She'd never been with a man she couldn't control with one icy look.

Good thing she wasn't interested in this man, then. Not even one little bit.

"All done," Kyle said softly, sitting back on his heels and zipping his bag. "Good as new."

With some amazement, she glanced down at her feet, wriggled her toes. The sharp, stinging pain had fled.

Sarah laughed. "Good job, Kyle. But I don't remember you being quite so kind to me."

"Of course not," he said wryly. "You were screaming so loudly, you couldn't hear a word I said to you."

Good-natured, Sarah laughed again. "In spite of that, you very bad man, I'm going to help you get the fire started." And she rambled off, leaving Katherine and Kyle alone.

Completely at ease, he smiled at her. "I put some padding beneath the Band-Aids so that your boots won't rub tomorrow. I have extra inner socks. You'll need to wear them under your heavy wool ones. Okay?"

She nodded, feeling strangely unable to speak. There were lines on his face, she saw, and they only made him seem more attractive, more rugged. Laugh lines. Already she knew the man laughed a lot. But why it made her tingle from the inside out, she couldn't guess.

"And I didn't even nick your pretty polish," he added, more than a little of that laughter in his voice now.

She wriggled her red toenails, beyond embarrassment. "Good. I would have had to send you my pedicure bill."

His next laugh held approval. "If you're so grateful, maybe you'd be interested in taking on dishes tonight for me—"

"Not a chance." But she looked at him from beneath sly lashes, hopeful. "Unless you have something magical in that bag for sore muscles too?"

The smile never left his face, but one brow rose, giving him a wicked look. "Not in my bag," he admitted. "But I give a mean massage." He lifted his fingers and waved them.

"Very slick," she said, nodding her head. "I bet that usually works too." Just his voice had her stomach turning to mush, but he didn't have to know that, thank God. And now that darkness was settling in, she'd lost her chance to go back today.

"Don't give up," he said quietly, still watching her, all amusement gone. "You can do it, you know."

"I don't know that I can, so how can you possibly know?"

He reached out and tugged her ponytail. "How long

has it been since you've done something without a court-room schedule, Counselor? Or done something new and unexpected for the simple joy of it?"

Lifting a shoulder, she pretended nonchalance, not easy when his eyes were on her, seeing more than she wanted him to see. "I don't have time for things like that."

"Here you will," he promised in that low, thrilling voice. "You'll have time for all sorts of incredible things."

What was incredible was what just his voice was doing to her insides.

"Give it a chance, Katy," he urged, tipping up her chin to look into her eyes. Because he seemed to see so much, she had the urge to shut them, but she didn't.

"Try living without a schedule, just for once. Do something because you want to, not because anyone says you should."

"I thought we have to follow the leader." Her voice was sharper, more sarcastic than she meant it to be. But having him so unexpectedly understand her was unsettling, as was his touch.

He only smiled at her gruffness, as if it amused him. "Only these first three days will be tough. Then we'll have a layover day at Dougherty Peak. You can relax at the lake, walk the creek, hike."

"Hike?" she asked horrified. "You'd *choose* to hike on your day off?"

His amusement lingered. "Some would. But you can do anything you want. We'll have several days like that. I'm not a slave driver, you know," he joked. "This is supposed to be fun."

"*Fun?*"

He laughed and shook his head. "Why are you really here, Katy? I've doubted that this was your choice."

"I told you, I'm on vacation."

"Somehow I picture a fully staffed cruise more your kind of thing than this."

"Mmmm," she said, closing her eyes. "With steak. Wine. A hot tub with boiling water . . ."

With lithe grace, he rose, grinning. "No hot tub, Counselor. No steak or wine either, I'm afraid. But you won't be disappointed, I promise." He went off, whistling, walking with that easy, surefooted gait toward Sarah and the fire.

Katherine let out a long, slow breath. Disappointed? No, definitely not. But the California cowboy had worked his magic on her after all, and despite her resolve, she'd fallen for it ridiculously—hook, line, and sinker.

THREE

The wilderness was not his thing. But to take down Katherine Wilson, he'd give it a try. He'd give anything a try.

He let them get a huge head start, which was only fair since he was so good.

In fact, he just might give her the entire first week. It would give her confidence, let her feel safe. Secure.

Then he'd move in for the fun.

Katherine Wilson, famed prosecutor and royal pain in his butt, was going down. Big time.

Nighttime, Katherine found, was long, cold, and more than a little terrifying. Kyle had set up four little double tents, and since Bettina and Chris, and Sarah and Jonathan took two, and Kyle took the third, she was alone.

Typically alone.

But this wasn't her cozy little apartment in the city. This was the untamed wilderness, where anything could and would go wrong. A bear could come roaming. Just the thought had her huddling deeper into her sleeping bag. Or, God forbid, a snake. She closed her eyes and told herself that little noise she heard couldn't possibly be anything other than the wind.

And that the fact that her entire body suddenly itched didn't mean she had bugs in her sleeping bag.

To sidetrack herself, she thought about the grueling hike Kyle had planned for the following day, and groaned aloud. She would like to kill that man, even if he was the finest-looking one she'd ever seen. Those eyes of his were warm, deep, and far too knowing. His body, that rangy, long, powerfully built body . . . she never knew a T-shirt could reveal more than cover, and that jeans, snug and faded, could so appeal.

He could cook too. The sloppy joes he made for dinner had been the best she'd ever tasted. Equally surprising, the man had done dishes, without fanfare. *Without a single complaint.*

Unusual, yes. But still far too laid-back. She'd never understand that wanderlust attitude that led him to roam about the wild for months at a time. It would drive her crazy. She wanted order, control. Regimented routine. It was what made her tick.

A soft hooting sound had her rigid in the bag. Then a coyote howled, or at least she thought it was a coyote. The cry had chills racing up her spine. If she'd had family, or even close friends, she might have thought about them now. But she didn't, so she closed her eyes.

But all she could see, suddenly, was poor Springer . . . dead.

And there was someone out there who wanted her the same way.

Another low hooting and she dove deep, burying her head under her arms as she gave in to the fear and prayed for morning.

Morning was Kyle's favorite time of the day. Rising early, he wandered off for some private time, some tranquillity. Sitting on a rock ledge overlooking the most gorgeous valley he'd ever seen, he watched the sun come up.

One more day and they'd be over Granite Pass, past the heaviest of their elevation gains. If Katy could make it today, she'd have no trouble after that. If she couldn't . . . Much as he didn't want to think about it, it was a distinct possibility. In a location as remote as this, there wasn't a road around.

Bottom line; he'd have to hike her back out the way they'd come. He and the others would lose two precious days.

"The Canyons of the Kings," as he liked to call this particular trail, was the one trek he got to make the least often. It was also his favorite. He'd hate to have to call it off, especially for one beautiful, spoiled woman he never should have agreed to take along in the first place.

A crunching of pine needles and fallen leaves alerted him that someone was coming, but he didn't need to turn to see her. Sensuous, expensive scent mixed exotically with the fragrant woods around him. "You're the only person I'd ever camped with that smells so good all the time," he murmured, inhaling deeply.

Carrying a toothbrush and a small bag, Katherine came up beside him, her eyes riveted on the sunrise he'd been admiring only a minute before. Her shiny blond hair was still loose and straight as a curtain to her shoulders. Her flannel shirt had not yet been buttoned over a snug, white ribbed tank top tucked into tight jeans that clearly outlined her long, willowy curves. "You're also the first camper to ever bring lipstick that matches her toenails."

She smiled, but he hadn't been joking. He licked his lips, shocked at the strength of his urge to rise up and nibble that color right off her mouth, and keep nibbling until her cool demeanor had blown away with the wind.

"I wanted to thank you." Tipping her head down, she waggled her booted feet. "With your first-aid and two pairs of socks, these dogs feel as good as new."

His gaze traveled down her mile-long, toned legs, and he had to swallow hard at the unaccustomed punch of arousal. Oh, he'd felt aroused before. Plenty of times. But never for a client, and certainly never for a woman as cool and aloof as this one. "I'm glad they feel good. We've got eight miles to go today, minimum."

Her gray eyes clouded with worry, but her mouth tightened with resolve. "No problem," she snapped.

There was that spark of temper again, the one he so enjoyed. But, man, did he still want to kiss her. "Are you sure? I don't want to have to carry you."

"I said I'm fine."

He smiled when she locked her jaw, spun on her heels, and walked away. Nope. There'd be no kissing for him today, he was fairly certain. But he was still going to have fun.

———◆———◆———

As Katherine trudged up the steep trail over the next exhausting hours, she felt a sense of sheer exhilaration and a deep sense of accomplishment.

On the crest of a river gorge, she discovered a high that took her a tiny step closer to believing in Kyle's way of life. A very tiny step. Because she would have paid a thousand dollars for a real hot bubble bath.

Every once in a while, when her legs begged her to quit, she'd ruthlessly remind herself why she was there in the first place.

To save her life.

That thought provided the motivation she needed to go on. But only several hours into the hike, she lost her second wind and seriously wanted to lie down and cry. Kyle, pushing up his sunglasses, gave her a slow, knowing smile.

Letting the others pass them on the narrow trail, he moved up right behind her. "Need a break?" he asked quietly so no one else could hear. There was no amusement in his voice, and she realized she'd sorely misjudged him. His friendly smile had been just that—friendly. And caring.

"I'll wait with you," he added.

He'd obviously sensed her unease in being completely alone on the trail. With an effort, she managed to answer without huffing too loudly. "I'm okay."

"You're really doing great," he murmured a minute later, after she'd tripped over her own two feet three times in a row. "We've come nearly four miles already."

Only halfway. If she'd had the breath, she would have

groaned, then cursed him. At least she'd stopped jumping at her own shadow, convinced it was Mohany. No one would ever find her so far out in the wilderness. But still, the thought, as always, brought back the nightmare she'd found on her porch at home.

She must have made a noise, given him some sound of her distress. "What is it, Katy?" he asked, tugging on her elbow until she stopped.

She said nothing and he just looked at her. "Something out here scares you." He looked around, at the trees, the rocks, the endless sky. "But what, I can't imagine."

"I'm not frightened," she said with bravado, turning to walk again. "Just in pathetic shape, that's all."

"That body's in shape," he said huskily. "And the only thing pathetic about it is what it does to me when I'm walking behind it."

"Then maybe we should switch spots." Her voice had lowered, too, though she hadn't planned on it sounding so whispery.

"I don't think it will matter much." His mouth twisted wryly.

"You're not . . . flirting with me."

"If I am, are you going to prosecute me?"

How she wanted to have a quick retort for him, but her tongue wasn't working too well. If she'd only been in the city, she assured herself, she would have been able to handle him as she did all men. Coolly. Lethally. Yet they weren't in her element, but the farthest thing from it, surrounded by nothing but trees and a thinning altitude that had, apparently, gone straight to her head. "I'd rather know how close we are to the top."

"Close enough, I suspect."

"You mean you don't know?" she asked as she stopped, horrified.

"Not really."

She felt her mouth gape open in shock, but couldn't help herself. "Don't you have a map?"

He laughed. "If I said no, would you fly into a temper?"

He'd like that, she realized. "Tell me you know where we are." The only thing that could make the nightmare her life had turned into any worse would be to get lost in the Sierras.

"We're in Kings Canyon."

Even she knew the canyon was so huge and so remote, they could wander for weeks without being found. She crossed her arms and stared at him, her chest heaving with exertion. "I . . . am not . . . amused. *How much further?*" She was so tired, she wanted to collapse, but couldn't stand the thought of giving him the pleasure of watching.

He grinned. "I could ask the others to stop now, if you wanted. We could just camp here if everyone agrees."

"You mean . . . you don't have a plan? A designated spot to camp tonight?"

That insufferable grin didn't fade as he studied her. "You're pretty hooked on schedules, aren't you, Counselor? Don't you ever relax?"

"This is the wilderness," she pointed out roughly. "I would think a schedule would be necessary."

"A schedule is exactly what we don't need. We're here for fun. If we want to camp here"—he pointed to a small clearing surrounded by beautiful ferns—"we will. Or we can camp there." Now he gestured to the next high peak. "What does it matter, as long as we're enjoying ourselves?"

"It matters," she grated, stunned that he couldn't see why.

"Because you think we're lost?"

So what if she was a fanatic about her time and how she spent it? So what if she had to know exactly where they were and where they were going? So what if she had to know what was going to happen every moment of her day? After what she'd been through lately, it seemed like such a small thing to ask of him.

Slowly his grin faded as he studied her. "I know where we are, Katy."

She didn't know if she believed him. After all, he took some sick pleasure in teasing her. "Okay."

"I really do," he added gently, nudging her into action with a hand to the small of her back. "Climb over the last steep hump up ahead, and I'll prove it to you."

The warmth of his hand went straight through her clothes. Again, that current bounced between them, the one that made her so inexplicably aware of him. Forcing her legs into action, she moved, but his hand remained.

"You can do it," she thought she heard him whisper, but she couldn't be sure of anything except her own harsh breathing.

After only three more steps she wanted to lie down and die. She'd humiliate herself, true, but she couldn't care. She was simply too tired. "Kyle," she whispered, about to humble herself completely and admit she couldn't take another step. "I—"

"Look," he said, pointing.

"What?"

Again, he gently nudged her forward with his hand on her back. "Up ahead, you'll see it in a minute."

But she couldn't, she wanted to tell him. She just couldn't.

"Almost there," he said again, his hand providing a wonderful support as she trudged along. "You're doing so well, Katy. So well."

She glanced at him, wondering if he knew how close she was to giving up. His eyes met hers. "You never told me what's frightening you."

"No." It was all she could say.

"So you admit something is."

With a nervous little laugh, she scrambled up a steep part of the trail. Over her shoulder, she said, "You're . . . pushing . . . now."

"Am I?" He smiled. "Better watch where you're going, Legs."

But she'd already stopped, shocked.

They'd made it to the top.

Below lay a spectacular canyon, where rock jutted straight up into the brilliant blue sky for what seemed like miles.

Katherine laughed as she panted for breath, and she turned to him feeling exuberantly alive. "I made it!"

"Of course you did."

"No," she said with a gasp, dropping her pack, "you don't understand. . . . I *really* made it."

"I knew you would," he said with confidence.

He did understand. He knew how close she'd come to giving up, he just hadn't let her do it.

Now she had something besides her own macabre thoughts to think about for a while.

That night, Kyle cooked spaghetti with a marinara sauce to die for. Then, brushing off offers to help, he cleaned up and handled the dishes.

Not the actions of a lazy cowboy, Katherine thought.

He looked up and caught her watching him.

"What?" he asked with a little smile.

"Nothing."

There's nothing sexier than a man washing dishes.

The next time he looked at her, his smile was gone and his eyes were hot.

"It's a full moon," Chris announced, then leered at Bettina. She giggled. In the next minute they'd both disappeared.

"Thought you said not to stray too far at night," Jonathan noted dryly.

Kyle laughed. "I bet they haven't strayed further than their tent." Drying his hands, he tipped his head back and studied the huge white moon. "It is a beauty. Can you imagine how it'll look down over the creek?"

"I'm getting my camera," Sarah said gleefully, stopping to spontaneously throw her arms around Kyle. "This is a wonderful trip."

Kyle laughed and squeezed her back. "I know. And it's just begun. Get your camera."

Katherine told herself she could care less who the cowboy hugged, as long as he got her back alive.

"You coming?"

Would her heart ever stop leaping when he spoke to

her in that low, deep voice? "No. I'm tired." Tired was actually a euphemism for near exhaustion. She'd found the emotional experience of the trial and what had happened afterward had finally caught up with her. Now the sleepless nights were taking their toll.

"Come on," he said, tugging on her hand until she turned around to look at him. The campfire set the red in his hair on fire and made his eyes glow with a warmth she firmly attributed to the flames. "Don't you feel well?"

"I'm stuffed." She patted her stomach. "You'll have to roll me to bed."

The way his eyes darkened, she imagined he'd get her there any way he could, if she was willing. *But she wasn't.* The last thing she wanted was a one-night stand, which is exactly what it would be. She had no time in her life for a commitment, especially to a man as different from herself as Kyle was, no matter how gorgeous.

"Just a little walk first."

She hesitated, hating to leave the safety of the campfire. She was acting silly, she reasoned. She'd been out there two days already. If Mohany had somehow managed to follow her, he'd have done the nasty deed already.

"You've got that look again," he said softly, and touched her cheek. "As if you're afraid."

She lifted her chin. "No."

"Well, then . . ." He lead her farther from the fire. "If you're not afraid . . ."

"Of course not."

"You'll have fun, I promise."

She wanted to protest, after all she could barely get one foot in front of the other, but in a matter of seconds they'd walked through the black woods and had arrived at the creek. The beauty of the night simply stole her breath away.

The moon was indeed full, and shining brilliantly down on the creek, lighting up the water with crystal points of silvery light. The trees disappeared into the night, dark shapes that vanished into the equally dark sky. The air around them was chilly, so she'd worn her parka. It reminded her to be thankful she wasn't in the hundred-degree heat of the city.

Across the way, she could make out Jonathan and Sarah, could hear the click of Sarah's camera shutter as she snapped the lovely night.

Kyle moved closer to the water and sat on a rock, gesturing next to him. She hesitated.

"I don't bite," he said solemnly, though his eyes twinkled. "Unless invited to do so, of course."

Remembering *she* was in control of this situation, not the incredibly sexy man laughing at her, she sank down next to him and sniffed haughtily. She imagined he rarely needed an invitation. Rather than encourage him, which would only lead her to disaster, she turned her head, stubbornly silent.

It would have intimidated every man she knew, but not Kyle.

"How often do you issue an invitation?" he asked in a quiet, throaty voice. "I bet not often."

"Let's put it this way." She met his amused gaze. "Don't hold your breath."

"You're something," he said with a laugh. "I bet you're the baby of a large family. And spoiled rotten."

"I don't have a family." She hated the way that

sounded, the way it begged for sympathy she didn't want, but it was too late to take the words back.

"None?" He went somber instantly. "What happened?"

She wasn't ready to share that information, or anything else about herself. "I think I'd rather hear your story."

He looked at her for a long moment while she held her breath, hoping he wouldn't push. "All right." He kicked back, leaning on his elbows. Lifting his chin, he studied the moon. "You may not be the baby of a large family, but I am."

"And spoiled rotten?" she finished for him with a smile. "Somehow, that doesn't surprise me. How many brothers and sisters do you have?"

"Six sisters," he said with a wry shake of his head. "And every one of them thinks it's their God-given right to tell me what to do. Can you imagine?"

She couldn't. The world she'd come from was too different. "And your parents?"

"Still spoil me." He grinned. "They still think of me as a little boy."

He wasn't little, and he certainly was no longer a boy, but she wasn't about to admit she'd noticed. *Six sisters.* What would that have been like? It sounded daunting . . . and wonderful.

"So tell me," he said quietly. "How did you come to be alone?"

Something about the way he said *alone* made her defensive. "It's not a bad thing. Actually, it's rather nice. No one to answer to."

"*How?*" he asked patiently, his eyes telling her he didn't believe one word.

"My parents were nearly fifty when I was born," she found herself saying. She had friends back home, people she'd known casually for years, who knew less about her than this man she'd met only two days before.

Where she gripped the rock at her sides, he ran a finger over her knuckles, loosening them until he could hold her hand. "An afterthought." He smiled. "A sweet blessing, in this case."

He nearly rendered her speechless with tenderness. *Nearly.* "I didn't realize you could ever consider an attorney *sweet.*"

Those lips of his quirked. "Not the attorney. *You.*"

Flustered, she continued. "By the time I was in high school, I was my parents' primary caretaker." She'd never forget those days; trying to fit law school, a full-time job, and taking care of her ailing parents in, all while struggling to make ends meet.

"You were still so young." His voice held far more compassion than she could handle.

"It was no big deal," she said with a careless shrug, tucking away the horrifying memories of watching them slowly die and having no one to help her. And being so damn afraid and alone. "They're both gone now."

"Isn't there anyone? An aunt, a cousin?"

It had taken her years to be ready to care so deeply again. She'd started slow. She'd started with a puppy. And now that puppy was dead. Murdered, to be exact. So she had his blood on her hands too. "I'm fine on my own," she said firmly, pulling her hand away, swallowing the huge, unexpected lump in her throat.

"And you're not married."

She had to laugh. "No, Mr. Subtle. I'm not married."

His grin was slow and far too sexy. "I'm not married either."

"Really?" she asked dryly, standing up in spite of her aching muscles. She had to put some distance between her and this man she suddenly wanted to kiss. "Not for a lack of offers, I'm sure."

"Careful," he said lightly. "You almost sound as if you care about my torrid past."

"Is it torrid?"

His low, husky laugh made her insides flutter. "Yeah. A little."

It was just enough of an answer to have her imagine all sorts of things—things that made her feel tingly and hot.

Craning her neck, she tried to see Sarah and Jonathan, but couldn't. Great. Under the full moon and clear, crisp air, she was quickly losing her inhibitions, and there was no one to stop her.

Suddenly he caught her shoulders in his two strong hands and pulled her gently back against his solid, warm chest. "Look," he whispered in her ear.

Her breath caught, but whether it was a reaction to the sight of the doe on the other side of the creek, frozen as she stared at them, or to the feel of Kyle's strong thighs bumping into the backs of hers, she had no idea. "Oh," she whispered, completely in awe of the beautiful sight. "It's Bambi!"

She felt his chest rumble with his chuckle. His hands softened on her until they felt like a caress. If she turned her head just a fraction, his lips would brush against her cheek.

Beep! Beep! Beep!

Bambi took off, leaping away into the night.

"What the hell?" Kyle's hands tightened on her as he whipped her around. "You're carrying a beeper!"

FOUR

Before Katherine could blink, Kyle had jerked open her parka. She opened her mouth to complain, but he slipped his hands in at her waist, then around, streaking down to the back pockets of her jeans.

"Hey!" she protested, shoving at his chest when those hands briefly cupped her.

Straightening, his face grim, he held up the confiscated beeper. "What is this?"

Reaching for it, she made a noise of frustration that she couldn't snag it away. She was tall, but not tall enough.

He turned and stalked away. She ran after him. "Wait!" She'd never been able to accept disapproval.

He didn't even slow and she began to panic. After all, the only person who would have beeped her was Ted, which meant he had something critical to tell her. So either Mohany had been caught, or— "Kyle!"

They reached a sharp drop in the creek, where the water fell twenty feet, crashing to the ravine below with a sound that echoed into the night. The scent of fresh water and fallen pine was strong. Somewhere, in the deep recesses of her mind, she was aware that she'd never seen a more beautiful spot. It didn't halt her growing consternation.

"What's the matter with you?" she demanded, coming up beside him. Automatically, she lowered her temper-filled voice in reverence to the awe-inspiring beauty around her. "Let me see the beep—"

"*This is the wilderness,*" he said, sweeping his arm out, encompassing all that they could see, which wasn't much in the dark. His voice was low and quiet in the night, but she had no problem detecting his disappointment. "The *true* wilderness."

"I'm well aware of that."

The disdain in his eyes dealt her a surprisingly tough blow. "Are you, Counselor?" he asked. "And are you aware that animals fight for their territory here. Sometimes with their very lives? Plants overgrow and strangle others to survive. Even this water battles the rocks and sediment for its path, pushing entire trees away to make its way."

She could see a huge fallen tree in the creek, the trunk at least ten feet in diameter. Water rushed past, over, beneath it, and in doing so, the course of the creek was changed forever.

He saw the beeper as an intrusion, she realized, and while she could understand, it didn't solve her dilemma.

He still held the thing, and she needed to see what it said. "Let me have it, Kyle."

"We're just intruders here, you know. We don't really

belong. Some of these trees are several thousand years old. *Thousands*, Katy. Can you imagine that?"

"Kyle—"

"This isn't our environment, and it's important to remember that."

"I haven't forgotten." *How could she?* She held out her hand for the pager.

"You scared that baby deer," he said quietly, turning his head to look at her, his eyes dark and fathomless. "Terrified it off into the hills."

"I want the beeper back."

His smile didn't reach his eyes. "Do you ever feel anything past your own needs, Counselor? Your own wants?"

That wasn't fair, and it more than hit below the belt. But Katherine was a professional at hiding her emotions, and she did it now automatically. Protectively. "What I bring on this trip is none of your business."

"You're wrong there," he said, moving to the edge of the little cliff. "I know this just burns your cute little prosecutor behind, but I'm in charge here. I approve what everyone brings, and that includes you. You neglected to tell me you had a pager, even when I told you in the beginning I expected you to leave it at home."

"I—"

He turned on her, but the shadows hid his expression from her, so she couldn't tell what he was thinking, until he spoke again. "For someone who's such a stickler for rules and regulations, you sure have very little respect for others. Is that because, as an attorney, you think you're better than me?"

"Are you comparing our jobs?" she asked, his anger

fueling her own. Why couldn't he just hand her the pager? If she didn't find out about Mohany, she was going to die of suspense. "A trek guide and a prosecuting attorney?"

"How ridiculous that would be," he said quietly, moving away from her.

She'd hurt his feelings. Again, she had to run to catch up with him as he strode away. Slipping a little on the uneven rocks and growth, she called out, "Wait, Kyle." He didn't slow. "All that I meant was—*dammit.*" She didn't duck her head in time and took a branch in the face.

Momentarily blinded, she took a step forward—and crashed into a hard, ungiving chest.

"All you meant," he said solemnly, even as he reached for her and tenderly brushed the hair from her face, "was that a job like mine couldn't possibly be as important as yours."

Well . . . okay, yeah. That's what she'd meant. But it was a fact, even if his touch made her wish that things were different. "Please let me see the pager."

With one last inscrutable look, Kyle turned and flung the pager as far as he could over the cliff and into the water.

With a sound of disbelief, Katherine rushed to the edge and watched as the flying piece of metal disappeared into the darkness. "No!" She whipped her head around and leveled him with a glare. "That was the most childish thing I've ever seen! *How could you?*"

He smiled then. "Easy."

Tears of frustration filled her eyes, but she blinked them back viciously. No way was she going to give him the satisfaction of seeing how much security that beeper had given her. No way would she let him know that now terror would overwhelm her, because she would have no contact with the outside world, no matter how flimsy or one-sided that contact had been.

She hadn't taken two steps away before he took her arm and tugged her around.

Just one more minute, she thought desperately, averting her face. Just one more minute, and she could have had her control back. But he always pushed too soon, too far. Saw too much.

"Hey," he said softly, lifting her chin with his fingers when she wouldn't look at him. "It was just a chunk of metal. It didn't belong here."

"You have no idea—" she bit off. Of course, he didn't. "Never mind. I'm going back to camp."

"Why? Have a mobile phone in your pack you have to use?"

How she wished. But with those warm hands on her, his eyes caressing her, and that low, mesmerizing voice, it was hard to remain indifferent, no matter that her pager was history. "You may be in charge of this trek, Kyle," she said, stepping back. "But I'd appreciate it if you'd stop . . ."

Now he bit back a smile as she fumbled for words, and she refused to let it bother her. "Stop flirting with me," she burst out.

"Stop flirting." He nodded his head as if he understood perfectly.

"And stop . . . talking to me more than the others."

"Is that all?" he asked politely, slipping his hands into his pockets.

No, she wanted to add. *Stop looking at me. Stop smiling. Stop everything, because you're far too sexy for my own good.* "That should do it."

"Fine, then." He came close again, flicked a finger over her cheek. "As long as you realize something important here. *I am in charge.*"

She took a deep breath, obviously prepared to object, but he placed a finger on her soft lips. "You agreed to go with me into this wilderness, Katy the Counselor, into this very remote, isolated heaven. I'm not certain why you did, but now you have to follow my rules."

He wanted to smile at the absolute defiance in her face then, but didn't. He had to make her understand. "This Sierra, this divine 'Range of Light' as John Muir called it, is an Eden of forests, streams, lakes, meadows, granite basins, and flower fields. The heart of it is legally protected from destruction or exploitation. Including," he added with an intense glare, "*obstructive noises.* I don't want any outside influences here. They simply don't belong. So you'd better make damn sure I don't find you on that phone you probably have hidden back in camp."

"I don't have a phone!" she said in an exploding whisper.

Now he did smile, in anticipation of watching her blow that icy disdain, that cool restraint. "But you wish you did."

Her eyes narrowed and he had to laugh. "Oh, yeah, you do. You'd have a helicopter here for you in no time flat, I bet."

Now her pretty, manicured hands fisted at her sides. "You think you understand, but you don't. I was expecting an important—oh, *never mind.*"

"Sorry you missed your boyfriend's call," he said in his friendly voice, ignoring the strange twist in his gut at the thought. "But this is the way it'll be out here. Since we've just barely begun, I hope you plan to at least *try* to enjoy the rest—" He broke off when she whirled away and stalked off.

He'd swear he saw smoke come out those petite little ears of hers, just before she disappeared in the bush. Whistling lightly, he followed her, uneasy that if he didn't, she'd never find her way back.

But less than five seconds later he stopped in surprise as she came barreling back out, flying at him, eyes wide, breath heaving.

"What?" he started, but ended on a big huff of air when she flung herself at him. He staggered a bit as her weight hit him full in the chest, but he managed to keep them both upright. As his arms came around her he discovered she was trembling violently. "Hey," he said softly in her hair, running a hand down over her quaking, slender back. "What's the matter?"

With a shuddery breath, she lifted her head. A scratch lined one side of her cheek, and he cupped her face in his hand to inspect it. To his further surprise, she closed her huge eyes and dropped her forehead to his chest, burrowing in as close as she could get.

Much as he wanted answers, having her firmly encased in his arms wasn't a bad thing. Actually, he decided as she gripped his jacket in two fists and held on for dear life, plastering the front of her body intimately to his, it wasn't a bad thing at all.

"I'm fine," she whispered, gulping. But she didn't move from him.

Holding her close, he murmured, "No, you're not. You're shaking like crazy." Her silky hair clung to his face, his mouth, but smelled so impossibly good, even in this wilderness of incredible smells, he didn't mind. "Tell me what's wrong."

She tried to pull back, and while he gentled his hold, he didn't let her go. Even in the dark he could see her discomfort, the two hot circles of humiliation on her face. Something had scared her, scared her good and deep, and he wanted to know what.

"Nothing's wrong," she said, still not looking at him. "I'm just being . . . silly. That's all."

With some admiration, he watched her pull a lid down on that growing panic he could only now sense. But what the hell had frightened her, he couldn't imagine. Reaching out, he touched her cheek and she nearly leaped out of her skin. "Awfully jumpy for someone who's just being silly," he said calmly, but his concern was growing. "You've hurt yourself dashing the way you did through the low brush."

"It's nothing."

"Do you know the only time I've ever seen you show any feeling at all is when you're terrified? I've seen that particular emotion several times now. Why?"

Her delicate nose lifted and she actually managed to stare him down over it. "Not all of us females have to be dependent, simpering, emotional wrecks."

"No," he agreed, "that's quite true. And I guess you'd consider a woman who can lean on someone once in a while weak. Wouldn't you?"

"I don't need to lean on you."

Now he gave her a small smile. "Everything is fine and nothing's wrong, huh?"

"I want to go back." She spared a quick, nervous look over her shoulder, making him realize that she didn't want to be alone. "You're the one in charge here, remember?" she said quickly. "So take me back."

He sighed. "You're not going to tell me a thing, are you?"

"Nothing to tell." But she stepped back from his touch, telling him plenty.

His touch did strange and unaccountable things to her. He should know. When he'd held her, something strange and unaccountable had happened to him too. No matter that he didn't have time for this sort of attraction, or that she was the complete opposite of the usual open, fun, laughing, and very sexual sort of woman he preferred.

He was attracted, deeply. But he accepted the knowledge with a light shrug, knowing that it would resolve itself. First of all, no matter if she was attracted to him or not, she basically thought very little of him and of what she thought he chose to do with his life. Of course, she really had no clue, and he had no intention of telling her the truth. Not when he was so very proud of Bonsai Trails. And second, they only had a little less than three weeks left together, then they'd go their separate ways.

They'd never have to see each other again.

The little lurch his heart took annoyed him.

Taking her hand, Kyle led her through the thicket of undergrowth back onto the small path that would take them to camp. She was silent and had mastered her emotions so thoroughly that he wondered if he would ever see her really let go.

Did she lose it while making love?

An image of her with her long, slim legs wrapped around him, her head thrown back, her breath panting in her throat, so staggered him, he nearly stumbled. Why was he suddenly fantasizing about this irritating, ornery woman he wasn't even sure he liked?

"Better get some sleep," he told her a little gruffly. "Tomorrow's our last heavy climb day. Then we'll take a day off to play."

She looked at him, her face half-hidden in the shadows, her eyes full of secrets. Still, unbelievably, she drew him. "I've read the itinerary."

So cool. So distant. So absolutely, stunningly beautiful in the moon's light. And if Katherine had ever indeed been frightened, which he knew she had, she'd managed to overcome it completely.

The minute they came within sight of camp, she dropped his hand and disappeared for the rest of the night in her tent.

The third day into the hike they climbed up and over Granite Pass. A difficult, strenuous climb, more due to elevation gain than anything else, it sapped every ounce of strength that Katherine had managed to retain through rigid anger.

Yes, she was still mad at Kyle. Furious was a better word.

All night long she'd lain awake, haunted by every sound, because she'd convinced herself that Ted had been trying to warn her about danger. By dawn's light, she'd firmly told herself it was impossible, that Mohany couldn't find her. But still, she leaped at every little sound as she struggled to dress in her tent. When she came out, angry, tired, and more nervous than she wanted to admit, the first person she saw was Kyle.

Casually, he leaned against a huge sequoia, cradling in his large hands a steaming mug of what she assumed to be his mouthwatering coffee. His booted feet were crossed, his long legs encased in snug, faded jeans that showed off their sinewy strength. Though he wore many layers on top in the chilly morning, T-shirt, flannel shirt, sweatshirt, she had no trouble detecting the power in those broad shoulders, in that wide chest. He looked, she thought with an uneasy ache in her middle, so perfectly suited to this rugged atmosphere, so capable, so very . . . splendid. She had to remind herself to be mad.

Judging by his knowing half smile, he knew it too. Yet he graciously brought her coffee, checked her gear, and inspected the scratch on her cheek, even when she was openly hostile.

"I told you last night, I was fine," she snapped. "And by now, I can certainly get my own gear together."

His smile pierced through the anger she was beginning to have to grasp onto tightly. "You've been out here for only two days, Katy."

"Katherine," she grated through her teeth.

His smile never faded, but now his eyes flickered with something that looked humiliatingly like humor. *At her expense.* "Two days does not an expert make. And for your information, your scratch is a little red. It's far too easy to

get an infection at this altitude. I'm going for some anti-
septic."

"You can go to hell."

Any other man would be either groveling at her feet
or running for cover. He did neither and it confused her.
Nope, he laughed. *Laughed.* And then got the damn anti-
septic anyway, placing it with a deceptive gentleness to
her cheek, blowing on it when she'd hissed out her breath
at the sting.

His soft breath on her skin stopped her cold. She felt a
deep burning within, all the way to her toes and directly
back up again, pooling uncomfortably between her legs.

The man turned her on without even trying. No man
did that. She smacked his hands away and stalked off.

Thankfully, at breakfast, Kyle had announced they
would stop in State Lakes Camp for lunch. There they'd
find, *thank God*, real showers and real toilets. They would
take a long break there, he said amid cheers from Bettina
and Sarah, then go on to the other side of the lakes, where
they'd camp for the night.

The state park was everything Katherine could
have hoped for, minus one critical ingredient. *A phone.*
She scarfed down lunch—another wonderful, delicious
meal prepared by none other than Kyle himself. The food
was a total surprise and sometimes she thought she must
be dreaming, everything tasted so good. Seemed the California cowboy had some hidden talents. Didn't matter,
she told herself, she still didn't like him.

She showered as long as the hot water held out, not
nearly long enough in her opinion, then almost froze to

death trying to rinse the conditioner from her hair. She could hear the cheerful curses of Sarah from the next stall, while Bettina suffered in stoic silence. The three of them met in front of the one small square mirror over an even smaller sink.

Katherine was horrified at her reflection, which she hadn't seen in three long days. Her cheeks were red from the wind and sun. Her eyes were bare of the protective cover of makeup she liked to hide behind. And her hair . . . it didn't bear thinking about.

Both Bettina and Sarah dug happily into the moisturizer she came up with, but teased her when she applied lipstick. It didn't matter to Katherine; she couldn't help the habit. But when she came out of the bathroom and caught Kyle's eye, she almost wished she had suppressed the urge.

His gaze, that light brown all-seeing gaze, dropped immediately to her lips. His own lips parted, leaving Katherine with the strange, insane urge to—*no*. No way had she just felt the pull of attraction, because it didn't exist. Her knees were suddenly weak because . . . she was tired.

Slowly, Kyle straightened, dropped the towel in his hands to the packs, and walked toward her. She had no idea what she expected as he came close; the confrontation that had been simmering between them ever since the night before, or maybe more gentle ribbing because she'd been the last to make it to the end of the trail. Her inexplicable anger at him had defused at his first glance, but she wanted it back. She didn't know how a man could inspire such anger with a quiet, reassuring voice and easy nature, but he could. He could as no other had before.

Without knowing why, she took a step back and wondered a little wildly where everyone else had disappeared to. Still, before she realized what he was doing, he'd backed her to a tree.

As he stood before her any more thinking became impossible. His hair was damp like hers, and he smelled incredible.

Slipping a hand under her hair at her nape, he fingered the wet strands. His other hand splayed over her waist, urging her to meet him halfway. Automatically, her hands went to his chest, to halt her motion, but her body had a mind of its own and somehow she ended up melded close. "Kyle, don't," she pleaded with her last ounce of resistance.

"Don't what?" he murmured, squeezing her waist gently.

"Don't . . . kiss me." She licked her lips, knowing it was an invitation but unable to help herself, her mouth felt so dry. He looked so tempting with his wet hair hanging over his forehead, his tanned face watching her so intently. And under her hands, which were still on his chest, he felt so magnificent. So warm. So hard. "I won't be able to resist you if you do."

"Why resist?"

That husky voice was going to undo her, and he hadn't even touched his sexy lips to hers yet. "It's not that simple. We're . . . different."

His thumb caressed her jaw, her neck, dipping low to touch the spot where her pulse tattooed a frantic beat. It was a struggle to continue to come up with reasons why he shouldn't kiss her when her eyes were crossed with lust. "We . . . don't like each other."

"I like you," he said, dipping his head so that his mouth hovered so tantalizingly close to her neck, she could feel his breath.

Her every muscle tensed in preparation for the feel of those lips. Her head even tilted a little, giving him access, but he didn't touch her. Not yet.

"I like you just fine," he whispered, and in the next instant, his mouth covered hers.

FIVE

Katherine tried to turn her head away, to tear her mouth from Kyle's, but he wouldn't allow it. In his arms, she forced herself to go pliant, not to respond. She kept her mouth tight and closed, but that didn't deter him. He nibbled, sucked, and stroked with his clever mouth and tongue, until with a small cry of defeat, she gave in.

He kissed her hard, deep, and heat surged through her body. So did a sharp, stabbing jolt of need, so intense, so wickedly fierce, her bones seemed to dissolve. She felt the bark of the tree against her shoulders, heard the sound of arousal he made deep in his throat, but could do nothing but hold on to him for dear life. She had no idea why she let him kiss her this way, but she did.

His arms were tight around her waist, crossed at the small of her back. But then his hold on her waist loosened so he could grasp her hips. His fingers kneaded her as she slid slowly down his body. When her hips rubbed over his, she felt the unmistakable bulge at the juncture of his thighs beneath the jeans he wore.

Her heart skipped a beat at the knowledge that she turned him on as much as he did her. When he cupped a breast, she gasped into his mouth and opened her eyes.

His fingers teased her nipple, and she bit her lip, dropping her gaze to watch his fingers on her.

With her last coherent thought she wondered what his fingers could do to the rest of her. What the hard, hot length of him against her, stirred by just their kisses, could do to her. She shivered at the thought and dragged his head back to hers.

Shamelessly, she wanted more, and he gave it. When he lifted his head again, she whispered his name in protest.

"We're going to have an audience in a minute," Kyle said softly. His chest rose and fell heavily.

The shocking reality that she was plastered to him like glue and that his hands had traveled up and over her entire body came to her then.

It made her moan helplessly.

"We'll have to finish this later," he whispered, reluctantly pulling back.

She didn't move. Had she ever felt so unbelievably aroused? So very aware?

His lips brushed her cheek. "You okay?"

Mortified at her response to him, she nodded and tried to back away, but all she managed to do was bump her head on the tree.

On the short trek toward State Lakes, Katherine found she had too much time to think. Jonathan, Chris, and Bettina had moved forward, leading, eager to move quickly. Kyle and Sarah remained quite a bit behind Katherine, discussing plants and environmental issues she didn't know anything about.

She learned that Kyle was a strong environmentalist, as was everyone else on the trip, and that they were all equally concerned about the overprotection from natural ground fires in this and other parks. Looking around, Katherine could see why. The thick foliage that had grown over the years was ripe for a vicious forest fire. Much of the slope they walked now was a thicket of young pines and mature brush. Some of the thickets were nearly impenetrable.

It was a huge fire hazard, and a great worry. She listened to them talk about what the management policy should be, to subject the primitive open forest to periodic controlled burning, or to wait and hope a huge, uncontrollable fire didn't destroy everything?

As Katherine listened to them talk she kept silent, awed by how much she'd taken for granted about this country's wild lands, and by how much she didn't know.

So she kept her sights ahead, despite their frequent attempts to draw her in. Even when the conversation turned casual and fun, she couldn't join the lighthearted banter, not when every time she looked at Kyle, she remembered his shocking, powerful kiss. There was no way to reconcile that irresistible, vital man with the one who had bossed her around the night before, tossing her pager into the waterfall as if it were a toy. It bugged her, his disregard for what was so critically important to her. She guessed that he had very little need for modern technology in his life, but it meant something to her.

Now she had no idea what was going on, or even if

she needed to be afraid. Painfully honest with herself at all times, she had to admit that for a long moment there, when she'd been locked in Kyle's very capable arms, she'd forgotten all about fear.

Her face flamed at the memory. Had he been as completely bowled over by that kiss as she had?

When she peeked over her shoulder, she locked eyes with him, since he was looking right at her. For a second neither of them moved. Then Katherine lifted her chin and gave him a cool, don't-try-it-again look.

His lips, the ones she'd loved to kiss, curved slightly. His eyes warmed. *Just wait*, they seemed to say. *Because there's more where that came from.*

She whipped her head around and kept her eyes firmly on the scenery. Not difficult to do when her view consisted of giant sequoias, so tall she had to crane her neck to see the tops, and such lush, breath-halting scenery even a firm city lover like herself had to give in and shake her head in awe. Now if only she could concentrate on the beauty instead of on the very likely fact that Mohany was looking for her.

She was watching her feet so intently, trying to keep the poor tired things moving, she crashed right into Chris, who had stopped ahead of her.

"I'm sorry," she mumbled as she lifted her head. "Oh!" Before her lay a huge, shimmering pair of lakes, surrounded by the famed sequoias that grew nowhere else on earth, and topped by an unsurpassably brilliant sky dotted with white cottony clouds. She'd never seen anything so lovely, and the knowledge that there was no other way to get there other than by trail gave her a huge sense of accomplishment.

"We're here," Kyle said, coming up behind them, dropping his pack, and looking excited. "Tonight we relax, we deserve it. Tomorrow, we explore!"

Katherine couldn't think past the need to get off her boots and plop herself down with exhaustion. She couldn't imagine *voluntarily* going off tomorrow on a hike that wasn't necessary, no matter how beautiful it was.

When Chris and Bettina actually had the energy to go off on a little trail they'd discovered, she could barely turn her head to watch them go. Then Jonathan wandered down to a waterfall whose tumbling waters they could hear.

Sarah sat down next to where Katherine lay sprawled back against a rock. "You look comfortable."

It would be too humbling to admit she couldn't have moved to save her life. "Very."

"Nice view." Sarah's eyes traveled to where, twenty-five yards away, Kyle was kneeling, building a small fire pit. With his every move, his wide shoulders stretched his shirt tight across tough muscle. His arms held a staggering load of wood, with apparently little effort. That face she loved to watch was intense with concentration.

"Is it?" Katherine managed to ask nonchalantly, though she'd been thinking that very thing.

"Are you going to tell me that body doesn't move you at all?" Sarah asked with disbelief.

Having been so rarely moved by something as simple as a male body, Katherine was a little disconcerted to admit exactly what watching Kyle did to her. Then he lifted his head and looked right at her.

Unbelievably, her stomach tightened, her breath

quickened, all from a look. Next to her, Sarah laughed softly, breaking the spell.

"Don't worry," she whispered. "I imagine he has that effect on every female he takes out here, he's so gorgeous."

Great. So she was to be lumped in under the heading *Stupid Enough to Fall for the Leader*. But she had to admit, if only to herself, that if Kyle had been anything other than a professional wanderer, she just might have been tempted.

She'd have to make sure to remind herself she wasn't tempted the next time he tried to kiss her.

That night, long after Chris and Bettina had made their excuses and dove into their tent with anticipatory grins on their faces, Kyle sat at the fire he'd built, sipping hot chocolate.

On the other side of the flames, Jonathan and Sarah were regaling Katherine with tales of their last trip, and she was listening, a small, warm smile lighting up her face.

Kyle wished she'd smile at him that way. She wouldn't, he knew. She didn't understand his world, so she didn't trust it. No matter that their kiss had set off shock waves inside both of them. She hadn't given in to those feelings easily. If he were smart, he'd think long and hard about even considering another kiss.

But from the moment he set his eyes on Katherine, he'd stopped thinking clearly. Yeah, she was uncomfortable in his favorite place—the outdoors. And the things that were so critical to her—control, routine, regimentation—were the very things he resented because they took away his freedom. Freedom from the tight and rigid responsibilities that plagued him most of the year.

In spite of her unbending, intolerant attitude, he was drawn to her. She had spirit and spunk. And she fought to keep her control in a place she couldn't possibly do it.

It all came down to one thing. He wanted her, badly. More than he could remember wanting a woman in a long time, if ever. Yet she didn't like him, or what she thought he stood for.

How easy it would be to tell her that he was the vice-president of a very successful international corporation. It would impress her, win her over—which was the exact reason why he couldn't tell her. He wanted her to like him for being just Kyle Spencer, Bonsai Trails. That was what was important to him, and that's what he wanted to be important to her.

When he looked at her again, he realized with surprise that she was sitting alone in front of the fire.

Unable to help himself, he stood and moved closer. "Everyone turn in?"

She nodded, her eyes seemingly huge in her face. The glow from the fire rested on her, emphasizing the light tan she'd gotten in the last few days, the way the sun had streaked her hair.

But when he sank down to the log next to her, he saw the telltale signs of exhaustion in the faint shadows beneath her eyes, the way she slumped on the wood. She didn't have lipstick on either, and that told him more than all the other things put together.

"Why don't you go to sleep?" he asked gently, nudging her with his shoulder. "You look tired."

"I'm fine."

He let out a little laugh at the icy tone, the absolute distance in her expression. "I think you'd tell me that even if you were dying."

"I *am* fine."

He took a good look at her, and realized something that bothered him a great deal. She wasn't just tired, but scared. He could see it in her cloudy gray eyes, in the tightness of her mouth, even in the way she held herself, with her arms wrapped around her middle. "Katy," he said softly, "won't you tell me what's bugging you?"

A ghost of a smile flirted with her mouth. "Maybe *you* are."

"You weren't saying that earlier," he reminded her, watching her flush a little at the reference to their kiss.

She gave him a startled look, as if she were surprised he could read her so well, before the mask of indifference dropped back on her face. "That was low."

"Sometimes goading you is the only way I get to see any emotion in your pretty face."

Another startled glance had him wondering if she had any idea how beautiful she really was. A woman who continually wore her claws and snarled at the world probably didn't allow too many people to get close to her. *Had* anyone ever told her?

"It's late," she said, rising. "I should turn in. Save my energy."

"Tomorrow you can do whatever you want." Though he knew that she, as the least conditioned of the group, needed the rest, he suddenly wanted to deter her. "You can swim in the lakes, walk the path along the granite basin . . . just smell the flowers."

In the distance, a wolf howled.

Her gaze darted nervously to the dark beyond their circle of fire. "I always wondered . . . are they like dogs?" She bit her lip, looking uncharacteristically open. "I mean, do they howl because they hear someone?"

"There's no one but us to hear."

"How—are you sure?"

She wasn't just nervous, but full of fear. Shaking with it. He tugged on her arm until she sat again, then with his hands on her, he turned her to face him. "Remember today, when we hit that state-run campsite? No one was there. That's because it's late September. Nearly out of season. Then, to get here, we went off-trail, *far* off-trail. That's because to me, cross-country travel is much more rewarding, and also where we're going is incredibly remote. Chances are, no one is within twenty miles, *at least*. Probably much, much more."

"But the wolf—"

"Is howling to his mate, the way he does every single night." Pushing back her hair, he studied her carefully, worry filling him. "Katy, please tell me what's frightening you."

She just stared at him, obviously trying desperately to regain her composure.

"Okay," he said evenly, knowing the more he pushed her, the more she'd retreat. "Then tell me why you came on this trip. It sure wasn't for pleasure." When she remained miserably mute, he voiced the thought that had been haunting him. "Are you running from something? *Someone?*"

The minute her gaze darted away, he knew he'd hit the jackpot. A well of unexpected protectiveness surged through him, so heavy, so fast, that for a minute he couldn't speak. He brought her face back to his and kept his voice low and calm, though it wasn't easy. "It's very unlikely we could have been followed. We didn't stay on the trail."

Her huge eyes blinked. "But it's possible."

Lying had never been an option for Kyle. It wasn't in his nature. "Yeah, it's possible." When she seemed to cringe and tried to turn away, he held her. "But it would take someone *extremely* talented in this sort of thing. Who are we dealing with?"

Her control was back. "I never said we're dealing with anyone."

"Dammit, don't." He gave her a little shake. "This is haunting you, so don't you dare belittle it."

Closing her eyes, she dropped her head to his chest, surprising him. It was the first time she'd voluntarily touched him. "I'm just so tired, Kyle," she said, her voice muffled against his jacket.

"And scared." He pictured an ex-boyfriend, stalking her, terrifying her, and he got angrier. So she could be difficult, impossible even. No one deserved to be so frightened.

"It's just that my imagination is on overdrive. I don't really know why. I just need some sleep, I think."

Automatically, his arms came up to hold her, but the minute they did, she straightened, giving him a wary look. "No."

"No?"

"Don't kiss me again," she begged softly. "Please."

When she looked at him that way, her eyes melting

with longing, need, hunger, he wanted to do anything she asked—anything except *not* kiss her.

"Something strange happens to me when you do," she added quietly. "I . . . lose myself. It's not very comforting."

Something strange happened to him, too, and it wasn't necessarily comfortable either.

Standing, she glanced at the tents, then back to him, uncertainly. "Do you think—oh, never mind."

There was no way he could resist her, not for long. But he stifled the urge to take her back into his arms, knowing she was too spooked. Oh, he wanted her, but he wanted her to want him back, to be fully aware of that wanting, not just trying to douse her fear. Rising, he took her hand. "Yes, I'll walk you to the tent. I'll even look under your pillow for the bogeyman, if it'll help you sleep better."

Her little smile, filled with gratitude, and more things than she knew, would have to be enough. For now.

Waiting outside until he knew she was asleep, Kyle moved his tent close to hers, angling it so he could see the opening. All night he slept lightly, half-aware, wanting to remain close if she needed him.

But she didn't.

The morning dawned with spectacular results. The few clouds that dotted the horizon reflected deep blues and reds as the sun rose up and over the granite basin to the east.

Katherine had never seen anything like it. Sarah, bubbling with enthusiasm, came up to her.

"Isn't it gorgeous?"

"It's not often I see the sunrise like this," Katherine admitted. "Most of my sunrises are spent in a brick building behind a desk."

"Check that out," Sarah said, pointing high above them and slightly to the south. A sheer granite face jutted out, topped by more sequoias. "Windy Ridge. Up on top is a meadow. I want to see it."

"You want—" Katherine glanced at the impossibly high ridge, then stared doubtfully at the woman she was beginning to consider her friend. "You're crazy."

"Jonathan's going to take me up. Chris and Bettina are going to come too."

"You're crazy," she repeated, craning her neck up the sharp mountain. "It's supposed to be our day off."

Sarah laughed. "Not *off*, silly woman. It's a day to enjoy your surroundings, do whatever you want to do." She pointed up. "And up there is where I want to be. Supposedly, when you're up there, you can stand among towering peaks, one mile above the lakes."

"Not just crazy, but completely out of your mind."

"I take it that means you're not interested."

"You've got that right. I plan on doing what you're *supposed* to do when you don't have to work. *Nothing.*"

But as Katherine watched the four of them take off for their goal of Windy Ridge, a small part of her sent out a little protest. *Should have tried it,* that little voice said. *It looks like quite an adventure.* But, she reminded herself grimly, adventure at this point meant staying alive.

"You could have done it," that quiet and deeply familiar voice said behind her. "You would have done great."

"Of course I would have." She forced herself to turn

slowly, to remain calm. It wasn't easy when just the sight of Kyle Spencer altered her pulse rate. "I just can't imagine why they'd choose to climb that mountain when tomorrow we're off on another three-day strenuous trek to God knows where."

He just looked at her. "Didn't sleep so good, huh?"

"Slept fine." But the compassion and understanding in his gaze was just too much to take to remain nice. "Don't you have something else to do other than stare at me?"

A wide, slow smile crossed his face. "I love how sweet you are in the mornings."

"Funny." But his sarcastic remark was close enough to the truth to have her squirming, especially when he didn't suitably back off as anyone else would have done. Instead, he seemed to see behind that wall she put up, and it was getting a little unsettling. "I'm sure you can find something to do."

"Yep. I'm going to take you to the lakes. We'll picnic and swim—nothing too strenuous. After all," he said, his grin turning a tad bit wicked, "I aim to please."

She could see him, that long, tanned, built body, in swimming trunks. All that bronzed muscle she imagined was there beneath his clothes, glimmering with drops of clear lake water. Just the thought had her heart hammering in her throat. "It's too cold to swim."

"Won't be by the time we get there." The speculative gleam in his eyes told her that he probably harbored high hopes of warming her up.

"Maybe I forgot my bathing suit."

His eyes went opaque. "You, ah . . ."

Well, she hadn't meant it like that, but . . . She smiled sweetly, enjoying his speechlessness.

"Maybe that won't matter," he offered finally, in a voice that sounded a little strangled.

Oh, no, she wasn't going to do this. Being alone with him for the day would bring nothing but danger, to her heart and soul. It was a cruel twist of fate that she was so hopelessly attached to a man she wouldn't let herself have. *"It matters."*

"Chicken." Now he smiled back, just as sweetly. "I'll show you where Butch Cassidy and the Sundance Kid used to hide out from the law more than a hundred years ago."

His vast knowledge had surprised her more than once. "You know so much."

"Not bad for a wanderer, huh." He shrugged. "I love history."

He was a man full of love, for a great many things. It appealed to her more than she wanted to admit. It also scared her to death.

"Come on," he said persuasively.

"I don't know." But that voice could probably cajole her into just about anything, if he put his mind to it.

"You could at least give it a try."

She could, and she thought with some surprise, she would. *But only because she didn't want to spend the day alone.*

They walked to the lakes in silence, a lovely, surprisingly easy trail that stretched Katherine's appreciation for the great outdoors. The trail was littered with fallen pines and leaves, the air buzzed with insects and birds. Squirrels chattered happily.

Still, Katherine remained a bit tense, braced for a barrage of questions she knew Kyle must have from the night before. Yet he didn't ask her a single one, didn't push for any conversation at all. Seemingly content with the quiet walk, he simply led the way, slowing as they climbed the last little ridge before they came to the lakes.

"Look." He pointed to a cliff, across the lakes, a quarter mile away. Standing on it, glowering fiercely, was a huge bighorn sheep.

She was grateful that the water separated them.

"The canyon is a sanctuary of bighorn sheep, deer, bear, and all sorts of other friendly critters."

"Friendly?" She didn't take her eyes off the sheep. "He doesn't look it." She had to scramble to keep up with her long-legged guide, who just laughed.

He stopped at the top, dropped his pack, and spread away some overgrowth with his arms to look down at the view. Katherine came up behind him, forced to admire his wide shoulders as they stretched, his taut arms as he held back the brush. With his arms lifted high holding the brush, she could see a strip of the sleek, bare skin of his lower back where his shirt had come untucked from his jeans.

"Wow," he whispered, still staring down at the water.

Wow was right, she thought dizzily. What was it about this man that sent her hormones into overdrive? She knew only one way to combat that; her famed chilly demeanor.

"It's all right." With her head held high against his incredulous stare, she walked right past him and down the path.

He didn't speak again until they were standing at the water's edge and he'd dropped his pack again. "Sorry this is all so mundane for you." With a jerky movement, he opened the gear and took a long drink of water.

Katherine's own mouth was parched, but now, at the sight of a single, cool drop of water making its lazy descent down the long column of Kyle's throat as he drank, she couldn't even swallow. She felt an insane urge to go up to him on tiptoes and lick that drop off.

She was falling for him more and more, she realized glumly, forcing her gaze away. But the only way she knew to handle this attraction was to annoy him thoroughly. "I'm just used to a bit more activity," she said coolly. "I don't usually have any downtime. It's been a while since I had a vacation, I've been so busy at work."

"Maybe you should take more time off, it might improve your disposition."

He'd spoken evenly, without a hint of sarcasm in his voice, but she felt it all the same. He didn't approve of her. Well, that was fine, because she didn't approve of him either. Not in the least. Plopping herself down, she tugged at the collar of her T-shirt, hating to tell him he'd been right about something.

It *was* hot enough to swim, and the water looked blue and wet and far too inviting. But to get in, she'd have to admit she *did* have a bathing suit, and that it was in her pack. She'd have to endure his knowing smile. Instead, she kept her back to Kyle and dipped her hands in the deliciously cool water, splashing her face to cool off.

Kyle walked a short distance away. He had a camera around his neck and was whistling lightly, completely ignoring her.

With him gone, she found herself letting go degree by degree. It was hard not to in the incredibly beautiful surroundings. She leaned back on her arms, her face tilted up to the sun, a sigh in her throat.

She couldn't remember ever feeling so . . . relaxed.

Until behind her, in the bushes, came a wild rustling, sudden enough to startle a scream from her throat.

He'd finally come, she thought dully, and her only thought was that because of her selfishness, Kyle was going to get hurt, maybe even killed.

SIX

At her scream, something red streaked out from beneath the bush—a fox. The body bunched and stretched as the fox ran hard and fast up the trail.

A fox.

Not a man with a leering grin and baseball bat. Not a dead precious little puppy. Just a fox.

Hunched over, on her hands and knees, she let out a harsh laugh. What a joke she was.

"Katy." The low concern, the urgency was there in his voice as Kyle dropped down beside her, slipping his arms around her waist. His breath was raspy, telling her that he'd run back to her as fast as he could.

It was tough, but she swallowed her ridiculous panic, pushed away from him, and sat back on her heels, shoving her hair out of her face. "It was a fox." She strove for a light tone. "This place is just plumb full of surprises, isn't it?"

He just looked at her. Still on his knees, his chest rose and fell harshly, which was interesting, given that the man could climb straight up five thousand feet of altitude without breaking a sweat. Did she do that to him?

"You screamed."

"The fox scared me?" she offered, but he just frowned, the darkest, fiercest scowl she'd ever seen cross his face.

"Oh, stop looking at me like that," she snapped, tired of being afraid and deciding she wouldn't be, ever again. "I'm fine. A little jumpy, that's all. Who wouldn't be, out here?"

His mouth tightened. She knew he took the insult personally, knew how he felt about the wilderness, and in truth, she was beginning to feel the same way. She thought she just might have fallen in love with blue skies, clear water, no smog. But she wasn't about to admit that, not to a man who made her wish for things that she'd never given a second thought to. Things like . . . having someone to care about, family . . . *love*.

She took a big gulp and an even bigger mental step back. *No way*, she told herself firmly, no way was she falling for this California cowboy who had nothing better to do than take people for nature walks.

Then, from beneath the same bush as the fox had streaked, came more rustling. Katherine put a hand to her heart.

When she saw the small black nose, the huge black eyes, set in a baby fox's tiny, rounded face, she melted from the inside out. A little red-and-white body emerged, followed by another, slightly smaller one. "Babies," she whispered. And it was everything she could do not to remember her own little puppy.

The foxes stared at the two humans from beneath the

edge of the bush, wriggling masses of adorable fur. One of them sniffed and whined, and Katherine felt a stinging behind her eyes. God, she missed Springer. "Oh, Kyle, look. We scared their mama off."

But Kyle's gaze was riveted to the enigmatic woman kneeling beside him, and the transformation that had just occurred in her. Her eyes had gone soft and dark gray, her shoulders had sagged slightly from their usual stiff and straight posture. Her expression didn't hold its usual cynicism, but something much softer, much warmer. No longer did she look like a tough prosecutor dressing down in jeans. She looked like a lovely, carefree woman, unbearably touched at the unexpected sight of the beauty of a wild animal.

She whirled to him, grabbing his hands. "Will she come back? Or do you think she's abandoned them?"

"She'll be back," he promised, stunned by the amazingly warm smile she shot him before darting her gaze back to the baby foxes.

"Are you sure?" she asked, not taking her eyes off the babies. "How do you know?"

It touched him, this desperate protectiveness she felt for the foxes, and suddenly that same emotion overcame him, *for her.* "She won't leave them, Katy. They're her life."

Again, she looked at him, and again, he was staggered by the first real sign of warmth he'd seen from her. Before, he'd been drawn to her on a purely physical level, a reaction to her sheer beauty and determination. Now, seeing the emotion she was capable of, realizing she did indeed have a heart, that it was just buried deep, his attraction grew.

"I wish I could hold one," she whispered, but he shook his head.

"They look adorable, I know, but they're wild. They'd bite if you came close." He cleared his throat and rubbed his thumbs over her hands, which still held his. When she looked at him, he shook his head again. "Do you have any idea how beautiful you are when you do that?" he asked softly.

"Do what?"

"Show the real Katherine Wilson."

Her gaze dropped and she tried to tug back her hands, but he held firm. "It's the first time," he said quietly.

"Not the first," she said, just as quietly. Uncomfortably, she shifted, and admitted, "When you kissed me . . ."

"Yeah," he said a little thickly, roughly, "I remember. But I dragged those emotions out of you, you weren't exactly willing and eager. This time you did it all on your own." And it was all the sweeter for that reason. "Look," he whispered, nodding his head toward the bush, which had started to wiggle again. The babies disappeared back beneath the greens. "She's come back in on the other side. They'll be okay now. She probably brought them food."

"I'm glad. I hate to think . . ." She hesitated and shot him a self-conscious look.

"You hate to think what?"

"I didn't want them to be all alone in this world, didn't want to think about them trying to fend off predators by themselves."

"Is that how it is for you, Katy? Do you think you're all alone, fighting off the predators?"

That must have hit a little too close to home for her, because she yanked her hands free and stood abruptly, walking to the water's edge. He sat back and watched her for a minute before rising to stand behind her.

"So defensive," he said lightly, touching her shoulders in anticipation of her flight. But she didn't budge; in fact, didn't move a muscle.

"You see right through me," she said in a low, bewildered voice. "I don't understand why. No one else ever does."

"Maybe I care more than the others."

Now she shrugged, and he could hear her genuine confusion. "But I've only just met you."

"Some things, sometimes the *best* things, come quickly." He turned her toward him. "There is something between us. You feel it, don't you?"

"I don't want to."

He laughed, feeling a little light-headed at her near admission. "But you do."

"Maybe. A little."

"Have you always been alone?" It bothered him to think that she had. He had a huge family, one that was incredibly close. Since he'd been given tons of attention, affection, and as much love as he wanted, it was hard to imagine going without it. But he knew this woman had, and he wanted to make it up to her.

"Since my parents died."

He suspected she'd been alone a lot before then as well. "Were you close?"

"As close as we could be."

Another cryptic answer, one that he'd have to decode. She never seemed to answer questions about herself straight out. "Were they there for you, when you needed them?"

She backed up a step, and he sensed her need for distance, which he'd give, to a point. "It was hard," she admitted. "They were so much older, and out of touch in so many ways. My father called me Katy. He was the only one."

"I call you Katy because it fits you," he said softly. "You are as pretty as the name. But if it reminds you of him and makes you sad, I'll stop."

"No." She gave him a little smile. "I think I've gotten used to it." Her eyes seemed unusually gray. "I can't imagine you calling me anything else."

"You were going to tell me about being a kid with parents so much older."

She looked away, broke eye contact. "Sometimes I felt alone because I had no one to talk to. Especially in high school."

The image that projected made him ache. "A tough age to have no one around."

"It made me different, or at least I *felt* different, from the other kids. Because of that, I didn't make a lot of friends."

"Yet you managed to get through, then go to law school as well. That's quite an accomplishment for someone on her own."

She gave him a self-conscious smile. "It wasn't easy, believe me. I worked two jobs and school was tough."

Not as tough as her. "You must have been popular."

Her pale eyebrows lifted in surprise. "Why would you think that?"

"Because you're beautiful."

She laughed. "They called me the Ice Queen." Her look was wry. "No . . . I wasn't particularly popular."

"You just scared them, that's all. They didn't understand you."

"No, they didn't."

"Didn't you have anyone?"

"No."

"Not even a pet?"

A spasm of pain crossed her face and she took a deep breath. "I had a puppy. Just recently. A cocker spaniel. I named her Springer."

The way her voice cracked slightly, the tortured gaze her eyes had taken on, had his stomach tightening in automatic response. He didn't want to ask but had to know. "*Had?*"

"She . . . died." Blinking away the emotion, she lifted her head. "It's no big deal. I didn't really have a chance to get attached."

Yes she had, he could sense it, but why she needed to deny it escaped him. She was afraid to admit how she'd felt about that dog. The question was, *why?* Because it would make her seem weak? Or because it had been so new and devastating to care for something? "I'm sorry, Katy. I lost my dog, Chance, just last year. We spent fifteen years together and I was crushed."

She nodded. "Sometimes people get too attached. I don't usually do that—" She looked up and frowned. "I have no idea why I'm telling you all this."

"Don't you?" He took her hands. "Because maybe you like me a little." She would have tugged them back, if he'd let her. "I like you too," he said with a little smile. "A little."

"No you don't. I'm an attorney, remember?"

"Well, I didn't say I like what you do. I said, I like *you*."

"They're one and the same. I'm Katherine, the attorney. You can't like just half of me."

"You only like half of me," he pointed out.

The sun beat down on them, lighting up her amused expression clearly. "No. I only like you half the time."

"Because I'm a wild, free-spirited, lazy, good-for-nothing soul."

"I never said you were good-for-nothing." Her lips, the ones he was dying to kiss again, curved invitingly. "And you forgot to mention your attitude."

He couldn't help but smile back. "What's wrong with my attitude?"

"Let's just say that you wouldn't make it in the business world."

That rankled, given that he *had* made it in the business world, very successfully. He opened his mouth to inform her so, but shut it again. It would be too easy, far too easy, to give in and tell her that he, too, had gone to college, that he had a master's degree. He also held a very respectable position in an international corporation. He imagined her eyes lighting up, her mouth softening . . . her heart letting him in. But, dammit, he didn't want it that way.

She had to like him for who he was, or it wouldn't work.

"But maybe . . ."

"Maybe what?" he pushed.

"Maybe you do have a *few* redeeming qualities," she admitted.

"Like?"

She hesitated.

"Oh, please, don't be shy now."

"You're . . ." She tilted her head down to study him, and she still held his hands. His body tightened immediately. "You're pretty well made," she finished diplomatically.

He laughed to hide his embarrassment. "Thanks. I think. That's the only good thing?"

"Well, you can cook."

"I do dishes too," he added helpfully. Then he tugged her closer so that their thighs brushed together. Letting go of her hands, he took her hips and directed them to his.

Her mouth opened, her breath caught. Her eyes darkened. "Oh, my."

"You have a few redeeming qualities yourself, Counselor."

"I do?" Her voice was soft, whispery. *Aroused.*

"Yeah. You make me hot."

She shrugged him off quickly and backed away. "I'm . . . hot too. Gotta cool off," she muttered, not looking at him. Bending, she unlaced her boots, yanked off her socks, wriggling her red-lacquered toes. Then she rolled up her jeans and walked into the water.

Grinning, he did the same. When he came upon her looking up at the mountains surrounding them, he tweaked her hair. "Easy to see why you're such a good lawyer. You evade questions real well."

"I never told you I was a *good* lawyer."

He knew she was, could remember hearing about her on the news. "Aren't you?"

Glancing at him from beneath her lashes, she gave him a cold, hard smile. "Yeah."

"You look like one when you smile that way." It made him uneasy enough to want to shake her out of it. He knew only one way to do that. "Come here."

Awareness flashed in those sharp, gray eyes, warming them. "Oh, no, you don't." She turned, sludging through the water away from him.

Taking her arm, he whirled her around, and got a face full of cold water for his efforts. "Hey!" he complained, letting go of her to wipe his face.

"Back off, Spencer," she warned, backing up herself. "When you've got that gleam in your eye, you're trouble waiting to happen. Stay away from me."

"What gleam?" he asked innocently. He swiped at his eyes and peered at her. Lord, she looked good, her hair shining brightly in the sun, that flush on her cheeks. Her T-shirt stretched nice and tight across her breasts. A wicked thought came to mind, something to do with getting that shirt nice and wet. As if her body could read his thoughts, her nipples hardened. His fingers itched to touch her, but she crossed her arms over her chest.

"That one," she said, pointing at him. "That look right there. It spells trouble."

"No, it doesn't, Katy," he said, completely without guile. He even added a harmless smile that he knew happened to work. "I just want to talk to you, that's all."

She snorted in a very unladylike manner and moved farther back. "Right. And—"

Her next words backed up in her throat as he grabbed her and pulled her close. As he expected, she struggled, her kicking feet splashing water up and over their legs.

Lifting her higher against him, he snaked one arm tight around her shoulders, the other low on her bottom. Tilting her sideways, he cradled her to him, rendering her just a little helpless. Nice fit, he thought as she wiggled.

"Don't you dare," she warned, flinging her arms around his neck.

"Don't I dare what?" Bringing his head close, he rubbed his nose to hers. "I think it's only fair to warn you, I don't respond to threats well."

"If you dunk me," she grated out, fisting her hands in his hair, "you're coming with me. That's a promise."

"Hmmm." He pretended to consider her promise, then shook his head slowly. "Not good enough." He bent his knees, dangling her inches above the water.

"Wait!" she screeched, closing her eyes and tensing in preparation for the cold water.

"I'm waiting. . . ." he sang when she didn't say anything else.

"Please don't dunk me?" She added one of those little sweet smiles he had so much trouble ignoring. But the thought of her in a wet, tight T-shirt had taken hold of him. It was a ridiculous man thing, he knew, but he couldn't beat back the beast. He had to see it.

"That was very sweet," he said regretfully. "But you've really been a pain in the royal behind this entire trip. I think I should. Just to teach you a lesson."

"No!" Now she practically crawled up his body, clinging and rubbing against him in a way that had him mighty worked up. "I'll get my clothes wet."

He laughed. "Yep. That's the idea."

"Put me down right this very minute."

"Ah, ah. I'm sure that's not a wise tone to be taking

with me right now." He squeezed her close, then again pretended to drop her, catching her an inch over the water.

She screamed. Then, when she didn't hit the water, her eyes narrowed. "Put . . . me . . . down."

"You got it." And he dropped her.

Sputtering, coughing, snarling, she rose up, then before he could even hoot once with laughter, she was on him.

As he went flying backward all he had time to think was that she didn't fight like a girl. That thought was confirmed when he felt the impact of her body on his, all wet, hot curves as she straddled him, sank her fingers into his hair, and held him under.

He laughed, then sucked in lake water, but still he didn't fight her. For a long minute he let her hold him, simply because he loved the feel of her hips stretched over his.

She yanked him up by the hair, and he gratefully drew in the mountain air. "Are you going to let me drown you?" she demanded.

"Why?" he teased, shaking his head as he sat in the shallow water. "Were you worried?"

A muffled scream of frustration shook her, and she grabbed his ears, obviously intending to dunk him again. But he grabbed her hips and she stilled, as if she had just realized their position.

She sat directly on his lap, thighs straddling him tightly enough that the apex of her legs ground into his painfully erect crotch. Yes, the water was cold, but it didn't seem to deter his arousal any. In fact, he thought with a grimace and a shift of his hips, his wet jeans were cutting off circulation to that very important area.

At that shift of his hips, her eyes heated and she made an involuntary movement of her own, sliding the heat between her legs over him. He groaned and gripped her hips harder.

"Don't move," he said hoarsely. "God, don't move."

"Why?" she whispered back.

"Jeans shrink when wet."

Her eyes widened and she scooted back, kneeling between his legs as he sat all the way up. The water reached their waist as they sat there, staring at each other, breathing heavily. Then his gaze fell to her shirt, and his eyes nearly bugged out of his head.

The thin white cotton was nearly nonexistent, it was so transparent. Her bra was white lace, also sheer, showing off her small, firm breasts to perfection. Her nipples were rock hard, and clearly visible, two rose-colored pointed nubs that made his mouth go dry. His poor body reacted violently, his erection leaping behind the tight confines of his wet, clinging jeans. "I have to take these off," he said in a strangled voice. "Before I hurt myself."

Her gaze dropped to the vee of his jeans, and she swallowed hard. "I guess we're going swimming after all."

Her voice sounded whispery, breathless, and he knew that she was as painfully aroused as he. Which was unbelievable considering they were still fully clothed and hadn't yet even touched each other. "No one else has ever done this to me," he told her, reaching for her.

"You're not telling me you've never . . ."

He let out a weak laugh. "Uh, no." He cupped her

face, pulled her close for a long, drawn-out kiss as he tried to explain with actions rather than words. Lifting his lips a fraction of an inch from hers, he said softly, "I meant no one has ever made me feel this way. Like I'm going to die if I don't have you."

In his arms, she went unnaturally still. "I don't want you to feel that way."

He was pushing her, and she was far from ready. "How about we go swimming?"

To his disappointment, she sank down into the water up to her chin, depriving him of the greatest view he'd ever had. "We *are* swimming."

"I never swim with my clothes on." Not to mention that his wet jeans were going to do some permanent damage if he didn't shuck them right away. He ripped his T-shirt off over his head and balled it up, tossing it to shore.

Katherine's gaze immediately fell to his bare chest, and he held his breath, feeling her stare as if it were her fingers caressing him. Water lapped at his belly button. The sun beat down on them. From the distance came the chattering of birds. Neither of them spoke. But when Katherine let out a shuddery breath and licked her lips, Kyle knew he had to move, because just watching her was undoing him.

Coming to his knees in the lake, he grimaced and unbuttoned his jeans. "These are killing me."

"You're—you're *not* going skinny-dipping."

"I'm not?" With a huge sigh of relief, he shoved his wet, soggy jeans down over his hips and kicked them off. They, too, were tossed to shore. "Wouldn't want to lose them," he explained with a grin. "Might be hard to convince the others this was innocent."

"Innocent?" She didn't sound like herself.

He laughed, feeling a little cocky. "What's the matter, Counselor? Never seen a man in his skivvies before?"

She did meet his gaze then. "You still have some on?"

Was that hope or disappointment in her voice? he wondered. As he walked on his knees in the water toward her, his smile grew when she backed up and shook her head. "Shy?" he asked with a laugh. "I thought you wanted to know what I was wearing?"

Just as he reached her she gasped, "No. I don't need to know. Really, I don't—" She gasped again when he snagged her hips and drew her against him. "I—*oh*."

"You're wearing too many clothes," he murmured, dipping down to kiss her neck. His hands went to her zipper, but she slapped them away and shoved back.

With a nervous glance at their surroundings, she said, "I can't take these off. Someone might come."

That she was right didn't deter him, since he was simply teasing her. He had no intention of taking her until she was much more willing, and even then he wanted it to be someplace a hell of a lot more private than the clearing. "Come on, Legs. Let's play. I'll show you what I got, you show me what you got."

Shaking her head, she let out a little laugh. "This may be funny to you, but I have no idea how I got this far with you. I can't believe we're in the water like this together, and I'm in my clothes and you're not."

"I *am*," he protested, standing. Water fell off him, revealing that he did indeed have something on—his Jockey shorts. That they were a light cotton, and clinging to him in a way that had her mouth falling open, only egged him on. "See?"

"I see," she managed in a choked voice, turning her back. "I think we should go. *Now.*"

"But we haven't even eaten."

Another funny noise escaped her and she stood, making her wobbly way out of the water. For a minute he just watched her go, enjoying the way her jeans were so tight when wet, how her hair seemed almost silver. As if she sensed his gaze, she turned back, and for a blessed second she forgot to cross her arms over her chest.

He stood riveted at the view of her tight, rounded breasts, so clearly revealed through the sheer white fabric. Her hard nipples poked straight out, as if begging for his touch.

He would beg to give it, but she made another sound and whirled from him, finally crossing her arms over herself.

With a groan of his own, he turned toward the deep water and dove in. He spent long minutes there in the cold lake, swimming until he felt his muscles quiver, until he knew he could face Katherine without wanting to jump her.

Sometime later he climbed from the water, convinced he was under control. He lifted his head, seeking her out. She'd stripped off her jeans, and they lay spread out on a rock, drying. Sitting on a fallen log, her face tipped up to the sun, wearing nothing more than a shirt so wet it might have been nonexistent and a skimpy pair of white lace panties, Katherine made quite a vision.

He'd thought he could handle himself, that he'd gotten a hold of his hormones, but in that instant, when he honed in on all that white, creamy skin and long, toned limbs, he lost the battle.

Katherine merely smiled her cold, knowing, attorney smile and gave him a look that clearly said, *Two can play this game.*

He wanted her, but that look she shot him was like a cold bucket of water in the face, accomplishing what swimming several miles had not done. There was no way he was going to make love with Katherine the Prosecutor. No, that would be far too chilly for his warm tastes.

He wanted Katy. The warm, compassionate, sensitive woman he'd seen glimpses of beneath the surface. And while it just might do serious damage to certain parts of his anatomy, he wouldn't touch her until he could be sure he had the right woman.

SEVEN

It was time. He'd let Katherine Wilson get her week's head start, now it was his turn.

He grinned, then laughed with the delight of it all. Finally, he could make his move, show Miss Prosecutor who she'd messed with.

First, he'd terrify her. Then maybe he'd torment her, show her a little of what he was capable of. Make real good and sure she knew who was after her and why.

Then, while she was begging for mercy, crying for her life, he'd kill her.

After that, he'd be on his way. They'd be calling him senator by the next election.

They followed the trail over a steep ascent to Marion Peak, the supposed gateway into the Lake Basin.

Time seemed to stand still. Cobwebs cleared from Katherine's mind, and a sense of calm overtook her. The wilderness canyon was so stunningly beautiful that she felt she'd left her world behind.

Everyone but her was excited to get to the peak. It was where their river-rafting trip would start.

To get there, they wandered a good portion of the time off-trail, which only meant that she tripped a good deal over her own clumsy feet, no matter how gorgeous the scenery.

She had no idea why she felt so out of sorts, so terribly nasty. Kyle had been good, treating her exactly as he did the others, with kind, generous support. Never once had he touched her in any way other than to occasionally help her over tough terrain, and never once in those two days had he tried to flirt with her. He certainly didn't kiss her.

It was damned unsettling to realize that she missed his advances, and she got the uneasy feeling he knew it.

She lifted her head and studied the trail. To the right was a deep drop-off, leading down to a meadow that could have been made in heaven, it was so green and beautiful. To her left was a steep rocky incline. Trees and heavy underbrush blocked her view too far forward, and though she couldn't see anyone, she knew she wasn't too far behind the group. Kyle didn't really like her to be last on the trail, but she'd wanted that today. She'd needed to be alone with her thoughts.

Still, even though he kept his distance, he'd slow on the trail occasionally until he caught sight of her. He'd wave and then continue on.

That was how she wanted it.

She sighed, unsure of what it was she truly wanted.

At least her nightmares had stopped, and she was completely convinced that she'd panicked over nothing.

That Ted, too, had panicked over nothing. Most likely, that page from him had been to tell her Mohany had been caught doing something stupid and was behind bars where he belonged. What a relief, she thought. Now the senator, Ted, and herself could all get back to a normal life.

If she could ever finish this trip.

But she had to admit, she was enjoying herself, much more than she would have thought possible. The mountain air was superb, the surroundings the most lush she'd ever seen. Even with the killer hikes, she'd never felt more alive, more . . . happy.

Now there was a startling thought. *Happy in the great outdoors.* Ted would laugh his head right off. She almost regretted knowing that all too soon she'd be back in the city, behind a desk.

"Quarter for your thoughts."

She smiled and turned to Kyle, who had slowed down to walk beside her. God, he was something to look at. That hair that was never really combed, those fun-loving eyes, his generous, sexy mouth, his wide, muscular shoulders, his flat stomach, his long, powerful legs.

"A quarter, huh? Why so much?"

"Because I have a feeling they're worth far more than a penny."

"You're right there," she murmured, forcing her gaze ahead so she didn't trip on the rough terrain. An image flashed through her mind, one of him standing in the lake, the water lapping at his calves. Clear drops beading on his tanned, sinewy body. Only a sheer cotton brief covering him. She'd never seen such a magnificently made male. "I think I'll keep the thoughts to myself for now." His ego didn't need another boost.

"That's no fun." He studied her for a long minute as their boots trampled the prefall foliage. "You're sleeping better."

Of course he would notice something like that. It was his job, that was all. Not necessarily personal interest, just a professional one. Why did that hurt? "Yes."

He smiled, but his usual spark, that usual heat in his eyes was gone. "Good. You look . . . well. Happy."

"You don't," she said bluntly.

His jaw tightened and he fell silent.

She let that go, not understanding why suddenly, after days of not needing any antacids, her stomach hurt. Or why it bothered her so much that he had backed off without a word or warning. Ever since they'd dunked each other in the lake, and she'd taunted him just as he'd taunted her, he'd left her alone.

"Tonight we'll stay at Simpson Meadows," he said. "There's a cabin there we'll use. Showers. Beds." He looked at her. "Just your style, I imagine."

"Does it have room service?" she quipped.

Though she'd truly only been joking, his eyes went flat. "Sorry to disappoint you."

"I'm not disappointed. Kyle—" She stopped, let out a disparaging noise. She was awful at this, simply awful. She could confront a criminal, an irritating defense attorney, even her neighbor. But not a man. Yet one look at his tense, unhappy face, and she knew she had to try. "I don't understand what happened between us," she whispered.

"Don't you?"

He didn't believe her. "No, I don't. Call me stupid, if

you want, but I really don't get it. Was I wrong when I assumed . . ." God, this was horribly awkward, and, of course, he didn't say a word, just let her stumble through it. "I thought you . . . sort of . . ." She sighed heavily, stopped, and faced him. "Dammit, I thought you liked me."

His head whipped around, the surprise on his face evident. "What does that have to do with anything?"

"I just want to understand."

He shrugged. "It's simple. You wanted space. I gave it to you. Now you're happy."

"So you *did* like me."

A grim smile touched his lips. "Is that what this is all about? You need your ego stroked?"

"Can't you just answer the question?" she cried, unbearably frustrated.

"Yes, I liked you," he grated out. "Still do. Satisfied?"

"Yes," she whispered. "Very." Without another word, she turned on her heels and started walking the path again.

He stared after her. "Wait a minute. Just wait a damn minute." But she didn't, and he had to run after her. "What does this all mean?"

She smiled. "I don't know. But I feel better."

"Well, I'm glad somebody does. I'm confused as hell."

She stopped again and gave him that poor, stupid male look that most women have perfected. "I thought maybe I insulted you at the lake."

"Why?"

Again, he got that look. "Because after that, you stopped . . ." She faltered slightly. "You took one look at me and . . . Because you stopped flirting with me."

"Do you mean to suggest that maybe, when I saw you dripping wet, stretched out on that rock, nearly nude, that I found you *un*attractive?" The idea was laughable, only she wasn't laughing, she was looking away. "*You do*," he said. "You actually think that."

"I don't know what to think."

He turned her back to him. "For the record, I think you're the most lovely woman I've ever set eyes on," he said quite honestly. "Inside and out."

"You never told me."

He would have thought a thousand men would have told her by now, and that she would be tired of hearing it. "I saw you there, with those wet clothes clinging to your perfect body, and I've never wanted anyone more in my life. Does that make it clear enough for you?"

"Quite." But her voice wasn't steady. "I didn't understand. I thought you weren't . . . attracted anymore."

"I told you—"

"I know. Now I get it."

"Good," he said with exasperation. "Because I don't understand at all. Can you share it?"

"Share what?" Bettina and Sarah had come back for them, curse their well-meaning hides.

Kyle wanted to swear with frustration, but he managed to smile instead. "What's up, ladies?"

"We're here!" Sarah cried, pointing. "I can see the cabin down there in the meadow. We got here so fast, we'll have the entire afternoon off."

"And I see water just beyond the cabin," Bettina added. "We can go swimming!"

Kyle looked at Katherine, who stared at him in return. He could have sworn her lips twitched, as if she were fighting back a smile. So she, too, hadn't been able to forget their last "swim."

"I'd love to," Sarah said. "I'm hot."

"Me too," Katherine said, still staring at Kyle. "I can't wait to use my bathing suit."

She walked off with Bettina and Sarah, the three of them striking quite a picture. Too bad only one caught his interest. The tall one in the middle, with the attitude.

What did she mean by making him confess he liked her, then backing off? Did she want him to keep his distance? Or could he go back to trying to worm his way into her good graces?

He wished he knew. But as he watched her walk a little bit in front of him, his eyes glued to the gentle swaying of her narrow hips, he had to admit the facts.

She'd snagged a piece of his heart, and no matter how unsuited they were, it wasn't going to be easy to get it back.

Their little chat had given Katherine the information she needed, she just didn't know what to do with it.

Yes, Kyle was still attracted to her. No, she hadn't scared him off as she had every male she'd ever met.

But he was the one man she wanted to scare off, wasn't he? After all, they came from different worlds. She couldn't imagine him happy in hers, and she knew for certain she wasn't cut out for his lifestyle for long.

So where did that leave them? Just where they were, she told herself. She should leave it alone.

And never kiss him again.

The cabin was everything she'd hoped for. A hot, long shower drove away any lingering uneasiness. So did the soft bed in the room she was sharing with Sarah. Luckily for all involved, there were three bedrooms, so Chris and Bettina had their own, which they gleefully took.

Instead of rolling her eyes or feeling disgust at how much they obviously relished an entire evening alone together in a bed, she found herself strangely envious.

With Jonathan still in his shower, and Sarah sitting outside watching the stars, Katherine watched Chris and Bettina share a long, hot kiss and then disappear into their room. She sighed, her body tingling at each pulse point. Then she turned.

Her gaze collided with Kyle's as he leaned against the front door.

"I know what you mean," he said in that low, intimate voice.

"I didn't say anything."

"You thought it. You wished that you were the one being held, being kissed, being loved. You wished you had someone to hold that way, someone to cling to all night long. You wished for it, just like I did."

She folded her arms over her chest, a silly, childish gesture, she knew, but she couldn't seem to help herself. He put her on the defensive. "You have no idea what I just thought."

His eyes on hers, he stepped closer, stopping a breath away. "Don't lie, Katy. It doesn't suit you."

Damn him for making her feel small, petty. Especially when he looked so good, smelled so clean and male. She could feel the heat from his body, and experienced such a pang of longing, she nearly cried with it. When he lifted a hand to her hair, she closed her eyes. "You're doing it again," she said softly, resisting the urge to grab him and hold on tight. "You're making me feel unsure, shaky. No one does that to me."

"I do."

"Well, I don't like it, nor your ego."

"Another lie. And my ego's just fine, unless you're standing on it."

She had to smile. "I don't do that."

"Don't you?" he murmured, slipping his hand beneath her hair to touch her neck. "You turn me upside down, Katy."

Since her eyes were closed, her every sense was heightened. When his lips brushed against her temple, she allowed herself to lean in to him, just a little. Just for a moment.

"Tell me what watching Chris and Bettina did to you."

She sighed. "You know what I felt, you just said so."

"You felt jealous," he whispered. "You long for the same thing . . . and so do I."

Jonathan came into the room, gave them a startled glance. "I'm sorry, didn't mean to intrude."

Easily, Kyle stepped back. She felt the loss of his body heat immediately, and missed his hand on her skin. "Don't be sorry," he said. "This is the living room, after all. We all share this space."

Still, Jonathan looked a little embarrassed. "The sag wagon will be here in the morning?"

Kyle nodded, and Katherine asked, "What's a sag wagon?"

"I have a crew that will drive in the raft we're going to use."

"And more food," Jonathan pointed out, looking hungry.

Kyle laughed. "And more food. Fresh stuff. We'll pack the food in chests on the raft and ride down the river for a few days. Then we'll meet up with the crew again to replace the raft with our bikes."

Unreasonable panic gripped her. "I thought we were in isolated territory. So remote there wasn't even a road. How will they get to us in a vehicle?"

Kyle gave her a strange look. "We were remote. To-day, when we descended through Simpson Meadow, we came close to I-80. We had to, to get more food and the raft."

"So we're close to civilization."

Jonathan laughed. "Lord, no. There's no civilization for hundreds of miles."

"But you just said—"

Kyle tilted his head as he studied her. "I said we came *close* to the road. We're not on it. My crew will four-wheel up to where we are. As soon as we get on the Kings River, we'll be back in distant, isolated country."

"I see." But it didn't ease her fluttering stomach. *Close to the road.* Anyone could find them tonight. So much for enjoying a good night's sleep in the bed.

"Thank goodness for that crew," Jonathan said with a laugh. "It's been a bitch to carry food for six people for this week. Can you imagine if we had to carry all of it, the food for the entire three weeks?"

"No," she said flatly. "I can't."

Kyle touched her cheek until she looked at him. "You okay?"

"Dandy." The what-ifs were killing her. "Do you take this trip often?"

"Several times over the summer, yes. Why?"

"How many times do you run into other groups?" Or single insane people tracking down their prosecuting attorney to kill them?

"Hardly ever. Like I said, we are in a really remote area. Not very many expeditions come this far. We came most of the way off-trail, remember?" He took her shoulders and peered down into her face. "What's this about, Counselor? I see something brewing back there." He lowered his voice. "Something that looks suspiciously like the fear I thought we banished."

"I'm fine." But she pulled away. Again, she was being ridiculous. Absolutely, positively ridiculous. And his hands felt far too good, far too comforting. It'd be so easy to lean into him, to let him kiss away her fear.

But he wasn't the right man and it wasn't the right time for her. He'd be gone and out of her life in no time at all. She didn't want to be left holding a broken heart. No one had done that to her yet, and she planned on keeping it that way.

"You don't look it," he said.

She could see the questions burning in his eyes, but with Jonathan standing there, there wasn't much he could say. "I'm tired. I think I'll turn in early."

As she turned away she steeled herself against the need and hunger in his gaze. Also had to steel her heart against the urge to give in to that look. But she was a big girl now, one who hadn't had a bed in a very long week.

She stripped down to leggings and a T-shirt and tried to make herself comfortable in the twin bed. In another time and place, it would have seemed too small, too hard, and far too bare. In this time and place, it was none of those things. It was the opposite, in fact. Deliciously soft compared with the ground she'd gotten used to, and the sheet and blanket felt like silk.

Only one problem remained—it seemed far too large for just her. She needed Kyle to fill it.

She awoke to chaos. The sag wagon had arrived, and so had her fate.

Sarah sat on the couch in the living room, her ankle propped up and covered in ice. She'd fallen out of the shower.

"Stupid," she said for the thousandth time, smashing her fist down on the couch beside her. "Stupid, stupid."

Jonathan paced the carpet before her, his red brows knitted tightly together.

Chris and Bettina had taken over breakfast duty while Kyle dealt with his staff and the new supplies. When he'd finished, he sank down before Sarah and lifted the ice. His expression didn't need words, but he tried to give them anyway.

"I'm so sorry," he said, his eyes brimming with emotion as he gave her a sympathetic glance. "There's just no way."

"There's always a way," Sarah said a little desperately.

Kyle shook his head, unusually solemn. "You can't do it, babe. You can't make it down that river."

"Yes, I can," she said urgently, gripping Kyle's upper arms, digging her short nails in. "I can, I promise."

"No." Again, he shook his head. "It's a bad sprain, Sarah. If you fell out and jarred it again . . . No. You can't risk it."

"I won't fall out."

He just looked at her. "Everyone falls out."

"Strap me in."

"And what about the biking? You know we're not talking about a lighthearted ride through the park."

At that reminder, she swore softly and plopped back against the couch. "Go away," she said. "Everyone go away and let me have my pathetic cry in peace."

Katherine ached for her. Her brother came close and put his hand on his sister's shoulder. "I'll take you back."

"Oh, no," she whispered, lifting her gaze to his. "You can't miss this."

"And I can't expect you to get home alone," he said firmly. "There's always next year."

Kyle nodded. "You can go back with the crew. I'm sorry, Sarah. I'll take you next year, okay?"

"What if you're already booked?" She sniffed and dropped her head into her hands.

"It'll work out," Kyle promised. "You'll get down that Kings River yet."

"It'll be just the four of us, then," Bettina said with a worried frown. "Can we handle the raft?"

Even Katherine realized it took at least two people who knew what they were doing, and Jonathan was the second rafting expert. Kyle glanced at Katherine, and she knew exactly what he was thinking—how big a burden would she be as the only novice? Could he handle both her safety and the burden of being the only one who knew how to work the raft?

She held her breath. What if he wanted to send her back early with Sarah and Jonathan? Could he force her to go? Of course he could. But if Mohany was the one hunting her, and if he hadn't been put away for something new, she was afraid it hadn't been enough time. The furor from the trial hadn't died down in just a week.

Was it safe?

Her stomach did a slow, hard roll.

But she needn't have fretted. Kyle was not the type to go back on his word or to give up easily. "We'll be fine," he said quietly, confidently, still looking at her. "The four of us will do just fine."

With only the four of them continuing on, she had an even bigger problem to chew on. Bettina and Chris were a very romantic couple. How many times would she and Kyle get left alone?

Bettina and Chris held hands as they hovered near Sarah, trying to offer comfort. Even from her distance, Katherine could feel the intenseness that existed between them. They enjoyed each other, and would escape together as often as possible, leaving her to be with Kyle.

Alone.

He'd kiss her again, and she didn't know how many more times she could resist him.

According to her raging hormones, even one time would be too many.

EIGHT

It hadn't been nearly as easy as he'd thought to track Katherine down.

So with no way of knowing exactly where she was, he'd been forced to follow the sag-wagon crew of Bonsai Trails through the wilderness for two days.

But eventually he'd hit pay dirt and find her. Yeah, that would be fun. His heart kicked into high gear in anticipation. Katherine's puppy had just been a warm-up. He was ready for more action. He couldn't wait.

Katherine said good-bye to Sarah and Jonathan, though it wasn't easy. She'd come to like them in the short time they'd been together. She was surprised at how much.

It was sad to see them go, especially since Sarah had wanted so desperately to finish this trek. While Bettina and Chris prepared to enjoy their rest day before the raft portion of the trip, and Kyle was busy checking over and preparing supplies, Katherine got a little restless.

What she wouldn't give for a newspaper or a radio. Instead, she left the cabin, found a huge fallen log, and sat. The woods beckoned her, but coward that she was, she didn't want to leave the view of the cabin. Coming back so close to civilization had spooked her.

If Mohany was clever, he could have followed Kyle's staff. Oh, sure, she thought with a smirk. Ted would have just freely handed him out the information on where she was.

It was ridiculous. Her fear was completely unfounded.

Yet visions of a mutilated puppy haunted her.

"Katherine."

Gasping, she stood up and whirled in fright, then sagged back when she saw Kyle standing off to her side, watching her intently.

"I need to talk to you," he said.

Her heart was drumming so hard against her ribs, she failed to notice he'd called her by her real name, something he hadn't done since the first day. "You scared me."

"Why?"

He had her there. For just a minute she wished she could just be weak and simpering, fall into his arms, and cry out her nightmares.

"Why did I scare you?" he asked again, coming closer. "You know my voice, yet you nearly jumped out of your skin when I said hello. What were you thinking about?"

How screwed up her life was. "Nothing."

"You mean none of my business," he said, annoyed.

This called for a quick change in subject. "You're busy, I imagine, with all the things your crew brought."

His eyes narrowed, but he nodded.

"They didn't by any chance bring you any newspapers, or a radio, did they?" Even trying as hard as she could, she hadn't been able to keep the hopefulness out of her voice.

"Why?" he asked, giving her a long look. "Need to know something in particular?"

"Of course not," she said with a little nervous laugh. "I just—"

"Dammit," he exploded. Stalking to her, he grabbed her arms and yanked her against him. "Tell me what is going on." His low tone, his tense eyes, and tight jaw all combined to alarm her.

"You tell me."

Suddenly he let her go. Shoving ten fingers through his short brown hair, he turned away from her. "Never mind. I'll be busy getting ready for tomorrow. Stay close to the cabin."

Before he could get five feet away, she called out, "I thought we were encouraged to explore on our days off. Why should I stay close?"

Slowly he turned and pierced her with a hard stare. "I should be asking you that question, shouldn't I?" He made a face. "But I doubt you'd answer me. Just stick close, Counselor."

He knew something, she thought nervously. He knew something, and he was mad as hell that she hadn't told him.

❦ ———————— ❦

Kyle was mad all right, he was shaking with it. He'd just gotten his first look at a newspaper in over a week, one that his staff had thought to bring him.

At first he'd nearly missed it, the reference to the senator's son and how he'd disappeared after his trial. *Completely disappeared.*

Katherine Wilson had tried with all her power to put that psycho away, and now he was on the loose, not in contact with his parole officer or family. Sure explained her unreasonable fear, her reluctance to relax. But it didn't explain why she hadn't told him.

He'd thought maybe she had an ex in her past that was bothering her. Ha! He should have known his strong-willed, confident prosecutor wouldn't flip over something as trite as love.

God, he wanted to strangle her. Mingled with that fierce emotion was another, stronger one. He wanted to grab her, hold her tight, and keep her safe from harm. He couldn't stand the thought of something happening to her.

He went still, nearly stopped breathing. Had he just decided that she was to be part of his life, no matter what the outcome of this trip? That was a joke. She didn't even know who he was, and that was no one's fault but his own.

With a groan he dropped the rope he'd been working on since all he'd managed to do was hopelessly tangle it.

His first instinct was to march back to the prissy prosecutor and demand answers. But that would get him nowhere. Might even permanently scare her off. No, he had to try to get her to trust him, to open up and want to share her problems with him.

Kyle sighed and bent, reaching once again for the

rope. Before he could grasp it, a body smashed into his, knocking them both hard down to the ground.

"What the hell—" he started, then sucked in his breath sharply as Katherine scrambled over him, kneeing him.

"Not again," she whimpered, pawing him, crawling on him. The rest of her words were lost as she sobbed them unintelligibly.

He blinked the stars of pain from his eyes. "Katy," he murmured in concern, sitting up with her in his lap. "What happened?" She continued to gasp and pant and burrow herself in closer. Streaking his hands over her, he tried to figure out where she was hurt.

"No." Surging to her feet, she tugged at his hands, then his shirt. "Over . . . there." Chest rising and falling rapidly with distress, tears soaking her cheeks, she pointed, hands fisted in his shirt. "There."

"Katy—"

"It's there!" she nearly screamed. "Oh, God. My fault."

With one last uncomprehending look at her terrified face, he tried to go in the direction she'd pointed, but she made a choking sound and clung to him.

"Wait here." He had to pry her hands off his shirt, peel her body off his to walk back to the other side of the cabin, where he'd left her only a few minutes before. He could see the log where she'd been sitting. The sun beamed down into the small clearing.

He saw nothing out of the ordinary. Certainly nothing to frighten a woman nearly out of her wits.

Walking back to her, he was alarmed to see that she'd sunk to her knees in the dirt. With her hands covering her face, he couldn't see her expression, but her shoulders shook silently.

"Oh, God," she cried. "My fault. Again, my fault. I should have known."

Kyle went down beside her and carefully, firmly, took her into his arms.

At his first touch, she leaped up, searching his face. "Did you . . . find it?" Her words were unsteady, her breath harsh.

So encompassing was her fear, he almost didn't recognize the tousled woman in front of him. "Find what?"

Her smoky eyes closed, her face twisted. Without warning, she whirled and sprinted away. He followed her, not surprised when she came to an abrupt halt in the same clearing he'd just checked.

Face pale, eyes wide, she looked at him. He'd never seen such wordless terror. "God, Katy. What is it?"

"I'm losing it," she whispered. "Really losing it."

"No." He walked to her, took her icy hands in his. "You saw something. What was it?"

She closed her eyes, hiding from him.

"Katy." Gently he shook her, and when that didn't work, he forced her chin up. "Tell me."

"It was right there, at my feet. He . . . threw it at my feet."

Now he stiffened. "*He?* Did you see someone?"

"No. Just . . . the dead baby fox." Her eyes filled again, and they darkened to a color of clouds before a storm. "He'd beaten it to death, Kyle. Just like he did Springer." A single tear fell on his fingers. "I'm next," she whispered.

❖————————————❖

It took Kyle less than five minutes to discover what he already knew in his gut. He found no dead baby fox, and absolutely no sign of someone else in the woods.

In those few minutes Katherine had pulled herself together so completely, it had been shocking to witness.

But, he thought bitterly, she was a pro at that.

"Obviously, I was mistaken," she said coolly, the only sign of her distress in her slightly trembling hand as it smoothed the hair back from her face.

He whirled on her, where she sat serenely on the log. "Mistaken," he repeated darkly. "Really."

She nodded and didn't meet his gaze. "I'm sorry."

"You're not a woman given to hysterics, Katy. Yet just a few minutes ago you were hysterical. You thought you saw a murdered fox." He watched her swallow hard, then look at her hands, which twisted in her lap. "Why would someone murder a fox?"

"No one did."

"Don't play games. *Why?*"

She sighed and remained stubbornly mute.

So he was dealing with the counselor again, not Katy. Fine. He could play dirty too. "Who's Springer?"

She jerked as if he'd slapped her. "I told you. She was my puppy."

"You told me she died," he said in a carefully neutral voice, afraid to give away too much emotion. But his gut was churning at what he was beginning to suspect she'd been through. "You let me think it was something natural. You never said she was murdered, for God's sake."

"He bludgeoned her to death," she said quietly,

calmly, still staring at her hands. "At first I didn't know who, but then I read the note written in her blood. I'm to be next, it seems. Then I knew who I was dealing with."

"Wait a minute," he said, desperately trying to keep up. "Are you talking about the senator's son? The one you tried to send to prison for drug dealing?"

"Mohany. He's been threatening me. Ted, my boss—"

"The DA."

"Yes. He'd tried to keep it within the office because of what the furor was doing to his friend, the senator's, campaign."

"Screw the campaign," Kyle said crudely. "What about you? Why the hell weren't you protected?"

"No one thought it would be necessary." She swallowed hard. "Until I went home from work." Her careful, controlled voice cracked. "I found her, Kyle. She was on my porch, where she always was, waiting for me. Dead."

He swore, then sat his weak legs down and gathered her close.

"She was a gift. I'd never have bought myself a puppy. I didn't think I wanted her, but she . . . kind of grew on me." She clamped her mouth tight as if she weren't allowed to feel sorrow over the animal's death.

"Of course she grew on you," he whispered, stroking her rigid body.

"I've forced myself not to think about it." She gulped, hard, then slapped her hands over her mouth, trying to hold back her sob. "But sometimes I can't help it."

"It's okay to miss her," he said gently, while rage flowed through him for the person who had done this to her. And his anger wasn't entirely for Mohany, but for the fate that had left her on her own so long. "You're allowed to break down once in a while. You know that, don't you?"

Something in the way his hands held her, the deep, heavy concern in his eyes and his voice as he tried to soothe her, burst the dam she'd so carefully constructed around her heart. Raw, exposing grief gripped her, and when he murmured something sweet and loving in her ear, she lost it.

Harsh, wrenching sobs shook her, and all she could do was hold on and let the storm take her.

Kyle let her cry. He held her and stroked her in a rhythm that eventually broke through her haze and started to relax her tense muscles. The front of his T-shirt was soaked, stuck to her cheek, yet she still didn't move.

His heart, the one that was beating heavy and strong beneath her ear, felt so good, so reassuring, so life affirming. Eventually, she sniffed and wished for a tissue.

"Better?"

She nodded, embarrassed. When was the last time she so completely lost it? She couldn't remember. "I'm sorry," she whispered.

Cupping her face, he lifted it up to see into her eyes. "Don't ever be sorry for showing what you're feeling," he said fiercely. "*Never*. Do you understand?"

Helpless to resist the pull of those light brown eyes, she nodded.

"This wasn't your fault," he told her. "You didn't have the time to grieve, and you just bottled it up until you blew. But you do that with everything, Katy. You just hold it inside as if whatever you're thinking is something to be ashamed of. You're going to kill yourself that way, you'll just explode unless you learn to open up a little."

"It's not easy—"

"Bull," he said. "It's as easy or as hard as you make it. But you think no one will understand." He looked at her. "Or maybe you feel that there's no one worthy of sharing it with."

He meant himself, she realized. "We're different. I never said you weren't worthy."

"We're not all that different." He grabbed her hand and pressed it to his heart. "It beats, Katy, hard and fast. *For you.*" He curled his other hand around her waist and pulled her closer. Then he spread his fingers wide over her neck, sliding them down until they rested intimately above her breast. "Just the way yours beats for me."

It was hard to talk, much less think with his hand on her. "Now, that's a discussion we'll have to finish, because it's mighty important. But for now, we have something else to do." He stood.

She looked up at him, at his strong face, his broad shoulders. And she knew this man would protect her to the absolute best of his ability. "What?"

"First, check on Bettina and Chris. Then before we go down the river, we have some calls to make. We should check on Mohany's whereabouts, if they're known. Also, you should probably check in with your office, since I'm assuming the pager I tossed into the ravine was of little help."

"But there's no phone within—"

He gave her a little smile. "You never once asked me if I had a phone, Katy."

"You—"

"That's right," he said, nodding. "I have one. In my backpack."

Shock, disbelief, and an unbelievable surge of anger swam through her. "I can't believe you! All this time . . ." She had to close her mouth a minute, very afraid she'd say something she wouldn't be able to take back. Or that she'd start crying again and never be able to stop. "All those nights, when I was so scared . . ."

His eyes filled with a solemn tenderness she wasn't ready to face, so she whirled from him. Coming up right behind her, he said quietly, "Katy, you never told me, you never once explained. I thought you were just on vacation."

"You knew I wasn't."

"*I suspected*," he corrected. "But you never let me in. You never told me what was wrong. Believe me, if I'd have known, I would have told you about the phone."

"I can't believe it." Wearily, she bent her head, rubbed her eyes. A sound escaped her, a wordless, helpless, shocked laugh. "You've had a phone all along."

"You didn't really think I'd take five people out into the wilderness without a backup plan, did you?"

She had no idea what she'd thought, except nothing was as it seemed. "I'm not certain I trust my thoughts right now."

"I take my job very seriously." His voice was quiet, steely, and intensely intimate. "Despite what you think of what I do, Katy, this is tougher than it looks. Your safety, and the others' as well, is vital. This is rugged, unforgiving territory. I have to have a safety net."

"Hence the phone."

"Yes," he admitted. "Among other things. One of them being sharp instincts that I always trust."

"What are they telling you now?" she asked. "That your most inexperienced client is a loony?"

"That she's in deep trouble." Gently, he settled his hands on her shoulders, keeping them there even when she tried once to shrug them off. She stilled, too tired to fight him.

"The fox wasn't there," she whispered.

He didn't answer, just moved his strong fingers over her, working on the knots that had settled at the base of her neck.

She was losing her mind, picturing bloody animal images that weren't really there. "Kyle," she whispered softly, allowing her head to drop even farther forward, giving him better access, "do you think I'm losing it?"

For a minute he let his fingers work. Then he sighed. "No."

"But that—" She had to clench her teeth to keep her voice steady. "You didn't find what I saw—what I *thought* I saw."

His hands slipped around her waist, gently pulled her back against him. "That really isn't the issue here, Katy. Your safety is."

"Am I safe?"

His comforting hands on her tightened in a possessive gesture. "I'll make damn sure of it."

He would too. She knew enough about him to know that. It was ironic, she thought. The streetwise city girl trusting a country boy with her life. Yet she'd been in the wilderness for a week and hadn't once missed the city and its suffocating air. Hadn't once wished for the smell of car fumes or the rush of traffic in the evening.

And most disturbing of all, her California cowboy wasn't quite the lackadaisical man she'd thought.

Which made *him* the biggest danger to her of all.

Kyle brought Katherine the phone and she called Ted. He wasn't in, but she was able to speak to Stacey, his secretary. She informed Katherine that Mohany had been sighted in town several times, as recently as the previous day. But as an extra measure, Ted had a helicopter on full-time standby as close as the base camping ground where they'd started their expedition.

Katherine felt a great amount of encouragement and relief. Ted would come through for her no matter what. She could enjoy the rest of the trip without worry. Which, she discovered with some surprise, she wanted to do more than anything.

The great outdoors, it seemed, had grown on her.

Still, Chris and Bettina had to be told what they could be up against, and Katherine watched them carefully as Kyle told them about Mohany.

"I'm sorry," she said quietly when he was done.

Bettina reached for Katherine's hand, squeezing it tight. "Don't you dare be sorry. This isn't your fault."

"She's right," Chris interjected, smiling grimly. "And now that this trip has become a trip of survival as well as an expedition, we'll be ready. No one will catch us unawares. Right, Kyle?"

"No one," Kyle confirmed solemnly, nodding his head. "So we go on, then?"

"Yes," Bettina and Chris voted at once.

Gratitude and the unfamiliar rush of friendship flooded Katherine. Then, when she caught Kyle's warm and appraising gaze, her body heated even more. And it had nothing at all to do with friendship.

That night, as soon as Bettina and Chris retired with wicked grins to their bedroom, she was left in a quandary.

In order to avoid being alone with the man she couldn't resist, she needed to go to bed too. But to do that would mean to lie in a silent room next to Bettina and Chris's, and she might hear them.

She didn't think her libido could take that.

Biting her lip, she stood undecided in the living room, wondering what to do.

The low, soft laugh had her gritting her teeth. "What," she demanded as Kyle came close, "is so funny?"

"You." He stopped a breath away from her.

"I'm getting tired of supplying you with a source of amusement." Did he have to be so incredibly masculine, standing there in jeans and a dark T-shirt that clung to his strong, wide shoulders? She was tall, yet he towered over her, giving her at once a sense of security and a spurt of panic.

If he kissed her, she'd melt. She'd just dissolve into a liquid pool of longing.

He stepped closer and his gaze fell to her lips.

"Don't," she begged, shaking her head.

"I'm not laughing at you," he informed her. "I'm laughing *with* you. We're both sort of . . . stuck, wouldn't you say?" He glanced meaningfully at Chris and Bettina's closed bedroom door.

It was a vivid and uncomfortable reminder of several things. One, he no longer seemed to crave her as he had at first. And two, she felt this incredibly strong attraction only because he was the *wrong* man.

"You wouldn't by any chance have any earmuffs, would you?" she asked hopefully.

He grinned, a slow, wide sexy one that had her stomach tightening in response. "You do feel it," he murmured, taking that last step between them.

Now she had to tip her head back to see his face. "I feel nothing," she assured him, but her voice sounded whispery and breathless, even to her own ears. "I just want to get a good night's sleep."

"Why are you breathing heavy?"

"The altitude."

His chuckle told her he was on to her, far more than she would have liked. His knuckles brushed her jaw and she closed her eyes against the sudden onslaught of desire. "Well, then," he whispered, "don't let the bedbugs bite."

Confusion filled her. So did a hunger she couldn't have explained. "You're . . . flirting with me again."

"Am I?"

"It ended in disaster at the lake, remember?"

"I don't remember a disaster. A hard-on from hell, but definitely not a disaster."

Wrong time, wrong place, wrong man, she repeated to herself, over and over again, even as her knees weakened from his touch on her face. Once they got out of this wild place, the attraction would no longer exist, and even if it did, their worlds were so different, they could never survive it.

He would suffocate in her world, and she would in his.

A muffled moan sounded from the closed bedroom door, and Katherine felt it all the way to her soul. Muted pleasure and forbidden heat filled her as she pictured what was happening just a few feet away.

Heat suffused her and she looked down, mortified to be fantasizing this way, even more to be dreaming about a man who didn't really want *her*, but someone.

Kyle's hands cupped her face and forced it up. "Are you afraid?"

"No." It was the truth. With such heat and desire pumping her blood, there was no room for fear.

"Because you don't think he's coming for you?"

He still held her face, his thumbs playing over her jaw. She could feel each and every single pulse beat as it drummed beneath her skin. "Because of you," she managed.

Those eyes of his flared. "You need sleep. But first, this, I think." His lips came down on hers; hard, hot, and slow.

NINE

Katherine opened her mouth to take a deep, shaky breath, and Kyle's tongue plunged hotly, possessively inside. Her knees quivered, her body shuddered.

"Katy . . ." he murmured into her mouth. One hand ran down her back, jerking her against him while his other embedded itself into her hair and tilted her head back.

She found herself kissing him with wild abandon as he wrapped his arms around her and crushed her to him. When his wide, wonderfully warm hands cupped her bottom, pressing her against the hard bulge in his pants, she gasped.

Lifting his head, he looked at her through sexy, sleepy eyes. "I want you." His breath was warm against hers. His voice was low, ragged, and unbearably sexy.

She trembled and grabbed fistfuls of his short, thick hair, having never felt so hotly aroused in all her life—or so out of control. Oh, she wanted him, too, but not this way. She wanted it to be like the other relationships in her life, a diversion, a quick release, that's it.

Not this crazy, stirring, shattering heat that threatened both her heart and soul.

Gulping in a deep breath, she closed her eyes and forced herself to think of anything that would help her gain back a fraction of her control. Ice cubes. Multiplication tables. Ants. When it had worked, and she had regained some semblance of self, she looked up at him.

He was watching her carefully, for once his thoughts hidden behind an inscrutable expression. "That was fascinating," he said.

It wasn't hard to catch the slight sarcasm in his voice. "What was?"

"How you did that. Gathered yourself together. Really, your control is commendable." Extracting his hands from around her body, he gave her a hard, small smile. "Well, Counselor, good night."

Then he turned and walked away!

"Wait!" When he hesitated and glanced at her, she stumbled over her words like an idiot. "You said—I mean . . ." Her words trailed off helplessly. "I thought you wanted me," she managed to whisper.

His strong jaw was tight, his body stiff. Drawing in a harsh breath, he sighed. Torment blazed from his eyes. "I do."

"Then why are you . . ." God, this was difficult. And if her blood hadn't still been pumping wildly, if her body hadn't still trembled for his touch, she would have let it go. But she couldn't. "Why are you walking away?"

For a minute he just stared at her. Then, in one fluid

motion, he came back to her. Unable to stop herself, she reached for him, pressing close.

"I don't want to," he said with a groan, holding himself rigid from her, keeping his hands at his side.

"Then don't." She was shameless, she knew. But she couldn't help herself. She had to have him. She'd deal with the recriminations, the consequences, in the morning.

When she lifted her face, he took her mouth. The kiss was so devouring, so breathtakingly tender and sweet, she wanted to cry. His hands touched her then, pulling her close to that warm, hard body. His fingers came up to cup her breast. Through the layers of clothing she wore, she could feel his heat, his strength, and she arched her back, pressing herself further into his palm. He kissed her as if he could never get enough, while his fingers teased the hard peak of her breast.

Whimpers and meaningless words passed through her lips to his, and she was a goner. Forget control, forget holding herself back . . . she couldn't.

Then he let her go, simply let her go.

Staggering slightly, she stepped back until she encountered the wall. Scrambled thoughts jumbled hopelessly in her brain, but one stuck out. *He'd been the one to stop.* He'd stopped kissing her and was now staring at her, silent.

Yes, his breath seemed a bit harsh and choppy. And oh my, yes, he was still hard as stone, an impressive sight if she'd ever seen one. But *he'd* stopped, and she hadn't. That knowledge accomplished what thoughts of ice and bugs hadn't. It cooled her ardor.

"You lied," she said evenly, slipping her hands into

her pockets so he couldn't see them shake. "You don't really want me."

His smile was the coldest one she'd ever seen from him. "You're wrong, Counselor. So very wrong."

"Then why—"

"I want *Katy*," he said slowly, clearly, even if the words were grounded through his teeth. "Not *Katherine Wilson*." Turning, he walked to his bedroom door. Without glancing back around, he said, "Sleep well, Counselor. I'll be here if you need me."

After he shut the door on her, she stood there, stunned. Her body tingled, her insides yearned. She groaned out loud, closing her eyes and tipping her head back. She was needy and aching for a man who'd turned his back on her.

Kyle glanced at Bettina and Chris, who were suiting each other up in their life vests, laughing and kissing. Normally, their joy would be contagious, but his stomach was in such a tight coil, he found it hard to relax.

Hard. Now there was an interesting word, one that still, unfortunately, applied to him.

Shifting uncomfortably, he watched Katherine the Counselor make her way down the steep embankment to their makeshift dock. Because the day was already warm, she'd opted for shorts that showed off her mile-long legs and a ribbed tank top that drove him crazy. Beneath it, he could make out the outline of a bright red bathing suit.

It matched her lips.

With an inward groan, he forced himself to look away, made himself concentrate on getting the last of their gear into waterproof bags and into the raft. It didn't help. The minute she climbed in, he could smell her, that crazy, light scent of hers that wormed its way into his heart, making him all too aware of her whether he looked at her or not.

So he did. He looked right at her, found her watching him. Her eyes were unsettled, unsure, but her mouth was tight, unsmiling.

"Good morning," she said in that low, husky voice he loved.

Bettina and Chris welcomed her, but he couldn't bring himself to speak. Not yet, and certainly not in the next minute when she bent to drop her pack at his feet. Her light top gaped away from her, affording him a front-row seat of what he'd touched the night before.

His poor body went weak, and he had to sit down. With his shorts cutting into him painfully, his muscles quivering with rampant desire, and his mind tantalizing him with memories of what had happened the night before, Kyle's mood darkened.

"Kyle, how do you want us to sit?" Bettina asked.

"It doesn't matter," he said, forcing the sullenness out of his voice. "As long as Legs over there sits in the front."

"Legs" raised a cool eyebrow and wordlessly went to the front.

He relaxed, sat down in the back, and then they were off. For long blessed minutes he truly was able to put Katherine Wilson from his mind while he directed the raft down the quiet strip of the river.

As he worked the raft, he spoke to Chris, directing him in the use of the paddle, preparing him for the faster water. Bettina regaled them with hysterically funny stories of their last river trip, and Kyle found himself laughing right along with them.

The counselor remained silent.

The early sun beat down on them, the hum of wildlife was in the air. The lush green surroundings, the sound and smell of the deliciously cool water, all combined to soothe him, as only the outdoors could.

For the next several hours things remained calm and quiet. The current slid them gently past brilliantly colored cliffs, conditioning both heart and soul, giving him the first peace he'd had since the previous night.

They cut through the deepest canyon in North America on a clear mountain river with pure forests and white sandy beaches. It was rare, wild, and free . . . and it soothed him.

He knew it was the calm before a succession of "big hitters," or heavy rapids. From ahead came the roar of the white water that they couldn't yet see. "Batten down the hatches," he joked. "And hold on tight."

"Are we getting ready to crank?" Chris asked hopefully.

"Oh, yeah."

Without warning, the water quickened, rushing over rocks, ravaging plant life in its path. The raft fairly flew down the first series of little falls, and Kyle tightened his hold with his legs as he used the paddle to direct the raft where he wanted it to go.

Next to him came delighted and half-terrified peals of laughter from Bettina as the river took them thirty feet closer to sea level in less than a mile.

"Hold on," he called out, keeping his gaze straight ahead as he maneuvered them over the speeding water.

"We're not through yet." In tune to the shrieks and cheers from the gang, they made it through the first set of rapids.

When the water had turned relatively calm again, Kyle cast a look at his crew and laughed. All of them, himself included, were soaked to the bone.

"Fun?" he asked.

He got a resounding yes from Chris and Bettina, then looked expectantly at the woman who had remained quiet.

Their gazes collided, and as ridiculous as it sounded, time actually stopped. Since she was wearing both a helmet and a life preserver, and her wet hair was plastered to her face, it wasn't a sexual attraction he felt, but something much, much deeper. *Much scarier.*

"I loved it," she said solemnly, then just as suddenly she gave him a small, shy smile.

He could have whooped with joy.

Katy was back.

She lifted her hands from their hold on the seat. "That was a white-knuckler," she admitted, and everyone laughed. "What's so funny?" she asked, shoving her hair from her face.

"That was nothing," Chris told her, shaking his head. Water flew off him. "Wait until we really get going."

Even from the length of the raft, Kyle could see her pale a little. "You'll be fine," he promised. "But hold on tight. Here comes another set. We call this area 'Hell's Drop.'"

"Oh, great," she muttered. "I feel like a little kid on a roller-coaster ride."

"Everyone becomes a child on the river."

As he directed them, at times straining with each muscle to keep them on track, other times laughing out loud as Bettina shrieked and screamed, Kyle was painfully aware of Katy. So completely aware that he knew just when exhaustion hit her, when she was at the end of her rope.

He stopped for a break and served lunch in a gorgeous little meadow where wild ducks honked at them for crumbs. And because the rains had been slow in coming this year, when they took off in the afternoon again, they found themselves on a slow, enjoyable, lazy ride through the wild woods.

Everyone relaxed, including Kyle. So he couldn't keep from continually glancing at the serenely beautiful woman, the one who looked as far removed from the corporate ladder as she could get with her drenched clothes and matted hair. So he couldn't help but wonder when he'd get to kiss her again, or if they'd ever make love.

He could wonder all he wanted. As long as he remembered that in just over a week she'd go back to her world and he to his. For years, to the distress of his family, he'd been dodging *forever*, and the implications that went with it. A wife . . . children. Not that he had anything against either of those things, but he just hadn't felt himself to be in a rush.

Terrifyingly enough, he felt he was in one now. Knock it off, he told his aching heart. Katherine Wilson and Kyle Spencer weren't meant to be.

The day ended with a wild set of rapids that had everyone screaming. That night at the fire, they laughed and ate toasted marshmallows.

Kyle watched Katy's warm, animated face and ached even more, if that were possible.

On their second day, Katherine felt so much more relaxed, she even enjoyed herself. Before lunch, when the sun got hot and the water slow, Chris dunked Bettina.

Then Kyle dunked Chris and Chris dunked Kyle, and everyone was wet except her. Smug, she sat on the raft laughing until her sides hurt as she watched them play in the water.

Just as she realized Kyle had circled around behind to where she sat on the raft, she was yanked back against a very wet, very hard chest.

Water seeped into the back of her T-shirt, since she'd shucked off her life preserver. It should have made her cold, might have, except that the body against her was incredibly warm.

Kyle stood in the waist-high water, his arms around her waist. When she craned her neck at him, he was wearing a very wicked grin. "Don't even think about it—ahhh!" she screamed as she was plunged back with him into the cold water.

When she'd splashed her way to the surface, everyone was laughing hysterically. She had no choice but to join in—and splash Kyle in the face every chance she got.

Afterward, when the four of them had crawled exhausted on the shore and lay panting for breath, Chris announced, "I'm never going back to work."

Bettina laughed. "Right. You're just going to tell all your patients, the ones you've worked with for years and love almost as much as you love me, that you're giving up your practice."

"You're a doctor?" Katherine asked, surprised, sitting up and leaning on her elbows.

"The best," Bettina interjected. She flattened some high grass to get a good look at her husband, and they exchanged a long, sweet smile.

"I'd give it all up," he swore, "if I could have a job like Kyle's. This is the way life was meant to be lived."

A small smile crossed Kyle's lips, but he didn't speak. He just lay back in the grass, his head pillowed on his arms, watching the sky. *Utterly content.* That's how he looked, and Katherine imagined that's how he felt.

How often had she felt that way on the job? For that matter, how often had she laughed at work the way she had today? She hadn't laughed so much all year, she was sure. Yet with these people, three people she'd just met, she felt so at ease. She felt as if she had real friends.

The thought brought an unaccustomed lump to her throat.

"I wanted to thank you, Kyle," Bettina said softly, studying the sky. "This has been a fantastic trip."

"We're only halfway through it," he said easily.

"Even if I had to go home today," Chris said, "I'd be satisfied. This is really great, Kyle. What you do out here, what you do for us . . . you can't put a price on it."

But he had put a price on it, and people paid it. According to what she'd learned from Sarah, many people paid it, and some waited years to have the privilege of having Kyle Spencer as a guide. He was the best in the business, expertly trained. It showed.

Once again, Katherine looked at Kyle and felt . . . a

stirring of respect. It wasn't the first time she'd felt it, but it was the first time she could admit it to herself.

He worked hard, and he loved what he did. How many people could she say that about? "You'd really give up the city life?" she asked Chris, needing to know how a doctor, someone so highly educated, could consider giving it all up.

"In a heartbeat," he told her, perfectly serious.

"How about you?" she demanded of Bettina, knowing she worked for a fashion photographer. Bettina nodded.

"Are you telling me that you'd really not miss the city?" she demanded. "Not one little bit?"

"Maybe a little, tiny bit," Bettina admitted. "But only when I wanted a good shampoo or a thick, succulent steak."

"Wait until tonight," Kyle promised. "You won't have a single regret."

Bettina sighed. "You are a god."

"How about you, Katherine?" Chris asked. "You sound like you don't get it out here. Are you that attached to your city?"

Kyle tipped his head so he could see her answer. Their gazes met and she knew her answer was very important to him. It was important to her, too, important to make sure they both understood that whatever was happening between them was temporary. "Yes, I'm attached. My whole life is there."

"You mean the courthouse is there."

"Yes." Her eyes hadn't left Kyle's, and when he spoke, she didn't miss his tone of disapproval. It was in every line of his tense body, his blazing eyes.

"That's not an entire life."

"It's enough for me."

Bettina and Chris, obviously sensing the tension, rose and headed for the raft, tactfully leaving them alone.

Katherine, suddenly not interested in being alone with Kyle, started to rise also, but he reached for her arm.

"I'm sorry," he said in a low, husky voice. "I didn't mean to judge you."

"Didn't you?"

A soft sound escaped him and he sat up. He stretched, and his T-shirt, emblazoned with the slogan GO WITH THE FLOW, stretched also. Enticingly.

"I don't want to take away the joy of what we've done here," he said. "You weren't afraid once today. I watched. Please don't let me ruin this for you."

She hesitated, then shook her head. "You couldn't ruin this, Kyle. I did have fun."

"You sound a little surprised."

His hands were on her arms now, stroking, warming her from the inside out. "I *am* surprised. I didn't expect to enjoy anything so much. Not after . . . after I thought I'd seen that dead baby fox."

"You did see a baby fox."

"You believe me?" she breathed, closing her eyes for a minute.

"Of course I do."

"But you didn't see it."

"Doesn't mean you didn't." He shook his head at her expression. "I can't explain it either, and I hope we never have to."

"But you don't think I'm crazy." For some reason, that meant so much to her.

"Stop second-guessing yourself." For a minute his

hands tightened on her. "You're *not* going crazy, Katy. Not by a long shot. You've survived things most people wouldn't."

His faith in her was startling. And unbelievably touching. "I don't hate what you do," she blurted out. "I think you think I do. But I don't."

His lips twitched. "But you still don't approve." When she would have spoken, he placed his fingers on her lips. "No, don't say anything. You don't understand yet, that's all."

Then he replaced his fingers with his lips in a soft, devastatingly tender kiss. When he lifted his head, she had the most ridiculous urge to cling and beg for more.

Instead, she gave him her hand when he reached for it, and let him lead her back to the raft.

For the next few hours they rode hard and fast in an exhilarating ride that was like nothing Katherine had ever experienced before.

Then, just as Kyle was talking about finding a place to stop for the night, Katherine looked up into the heavily wooded edge of the river and saw a face watching them.

He leered and grinned.

She screamed.

TEN

Ah, he was finally getting to Katherine. Shaking her considerable control. Rattling her well-put-together guard. From the driver's seat of the Jeep he'd rented, he laughed. How many years had he waited for this opportunity? Too many. Because of that, she had nearly bested him.

She'd nearly, very nearly, gotten rid of him. Even she had no idea how close he'd come to losing everything—because of her.

It would never happen, not if he had his way. And he was going to make sure he did.

Yeah, he was scaring Katherine Wilson, and scaring her good. His only regret—that he hadn't brought a camera to record all the delicious fear.

But he wouldn't need a camera for his next trip. No, the finale would speak for itself.

And Katherine would never speak again.

Kyle stoked the fire and cast a worried glance in Katy's direction. She sat as he'd left her, huddled as close to the heat as she could get without scorching her skin.

His heart broke a little at the lingering terror on her face.

What the hell had she seen? And why wouldn't she tell him? Even Chris and Bettina had tried, repeatedly, to get her to speak, but she refused.

He walked back to her now, knelt before her, and took her icy hands in his. "Katy, tell me, baby. Tell me what you saw."

She shook her head and her sweet gray eyes filled.

"Please."

No answer. Nothing.

"Did you see him?" It was his greatest fear, that he wouldn't be able to keep her safe.

She shook her head and closed her eyes. One tear fell, and he caught it on the pad of his thumb.

"I'm losing it," she whispered hoarsely. "Really, really losing it."

"No," he denied, but she shook her head sharply.

"I keep seeing things that aren't there. I saw . . . a face. It grinned at me." She shivered. "It was a nasty, I'm-going-to-get-you grin."

His skin crawled. "Are you sure you imagined this? Let's call your office again."

"It's too late, they'll be gone." She sighed. "And yes, I'm imagining things. It's an awful thing to admit."

"You're not crazy."

Another sigh, this time one of exhaustion. "I need to go to sleep, Kyle."

He didn't want to let her go, but didn't see he had

much of a choice. She did look exhausted. Standing, he pulled her to her feet and walked with her to her tent. As she crawled in he bent down and made to follow, but she stopped him.

"I need to be alone."

"No, you don't."

When he would have pushed past her, she put a hand to his chest. "Please," she whispered. "Don't rush me on this."

He had to remind himself that this wasn't about what he wanted, but about what he wanted for *her*. He wanted her to feel safe, secure. He wanted her to be relaxed and carefree, as someone on a vacation should be.

He knew the roar of the river could lull one to sleep, could dance in one's dreams, could cause one to awaken in the morning with a new sense of being.

He hoped it would work for Katy.

He hated this insidious fear he knew she felt. Yet with those wide, cloudy eyes appealing to him, he had to give in.

"You've committed me to another sleepless night," he told her softly, touching her hair, wishing he could touch more. "I'll be in my tent, watching and worrying about you."

"Oh, Kyle." Her face fell, and he closed his eyes and sighed.

"Forget I said that." He lifted her hand to his lips and glided them over her knuckles. "Just try to get some sleep. You need it."

She nodded and shut the flap, closing him out of her tent and out of her heart.

❖————————❖

Normally, Kyle came awake in slow degrees. Not this time. He could tell by the complete darkness that it was very late. Or very early.

Wide-awake, his heart drummed a heavy beat in his chest. What had awakened him so abruptly?

Then it came again, a guttural, hoarse cry, and he was out of his bag and tent in a shot, diving into Katy's.

She was buried deep in her sleeping bag, tossing and turning, caught in the throes of a nightmare. She'd cried out again before he reached her.

"Katy." Heart in his throat, he lifted the pillow off her head and called her name again. She squeezed her eyes tightly closed and burrowed deeper. "Come on, baby, wake up."

He shook her and she moaned in fear. Beneath his hands, she trembled violently. Cursing, feeling the fear as if it were his own, he whipped off the sleeping bag and scooped her close. Smoothing back her hair, he kissed her temple, murmured softly to her. "It's all right," he said inanely, knowing it wasn't. "It's going to be all right now."

Still she made frightened little noises in her throat, and he rocked her back and forth as he tried to wake her up.

"He's going to get me," she cried, breathing as if she'd run a marathon.

The stark terror in her voice tore at his heart. The fact that she thought it possible ripped a hole in his gut. "No, he's not. I've got you."

"So much blood." A sob escaped. "Poor Springer, my poor baby."

Kyle felt a surge of pure, murderous rage for the man doing this to her. "You were dreaming, Katy." Smoothing back her hair, he tried to see her face. "Just a dream."

When she went rigid, he knew she'd finally woken up. "It's all right," he whispered again. "Just a dream."

Her eyes flew open, wide and dazed. Immediately, they shut again, but she curled against him, hands fisting on his shoulders, her breath still panting in her throat. He could feel her damp skin chilling, so he covered her with his body.

Big mistake.

She wore a T-shirt and not much else, allowing him to feel every curve and hollow of her incredible body. He'd been in a hurry to get to her, not stopping to dress, so all he wore was a pair of loose sweatpants. With nothing but thin cotton separating her chest from his, he could have died with pleasure right there.

When she shivered, she snuggled closer, plastering herself to him. Her heart still raced, he could feel it ricocheting against his. The hardened points of her nipples seared his skin. He heard his own harsh intake of breath, felt himself shudder in automatic response. Without thinking, his hands streaked over her, down her bare legs, and back up her taut thighs, over more soft, giving curves until he wrapped his arms tightly around her waist, binding her to him.

She shifted. "Kyle?"

"It's me."

"I—" She closed her eyes and quivered. "I had a bad dream."

"I know." He stroked her jaw, wishing he could make her open up to him. "I heard you cry out."

"You came."

"Of course I did. What did you dream about?"

"Nothing." Her voice sounded hoarse.

"More than nothing, I think."

"I don't want to talk."

God, that was trouble right there. Talking was all that was keeping him from ripping off her T-shirt and sampling what lay under it. Because he couldn't help himself, he dipped his head and tasted the delicate spot where her pulse raced at the base of her neck. "You're shaking."

At the touch of his lips, she jerked, made a strangled sound in her throat. Empowered by the knowledge that it was him making her heart soar now, not the lingering dream, he dragged his open mouth over her collarbone and nipped at her shoulder. "You're not alone anymore, Katy. I'm here."

She arched into him and made that low, needy sound again. The one that drove him crazy for her. He had to be closer, had to have more. Pushing her back, he leaned over her and slipped his thigh between her legs. She rubbed herself against him, letting him feel the heat of her. "God, Katy," he said with a groan.

"Make me forget," she whispered, cupping his face and pulling it up to hers. "Please, Kyle. Make me forget," she said against his lips.

Warning signals went off, blaring, screaming, but he was too far gone to do much about it. He couldn't stop now, not with her long, bare legs wrapped around his, her hands on his face, her lips on his. "Wait," he managed, lifting his head. "I don't want this to be just mindless sex—"

"Isn't that supposed to be my line?" she murmured. Letting out a wordless sound, she brought his face back to hers, raining kisses wherever she could reach. "I need to forget. You can make me."

"No." His voice was faint and rough with need. "Not like this." He lifted himself up on his elbows and stared down at her. "I want you, Katy. God, I want you. More than I've ever wanted anyone. But not like this. Not so you can lose yourself in me, and then when we're done, be back in total, cool, icy control."

Her hands smoothed down over his shoulders as she held his gaze, softly over his bare chest, slowly over his stomach muscles, which jerked under her fingers. They settled at the tie of his sweat bottoms, which were riding low on his hips.

"I want you," she whispered huskily.

God, he wanted to believe that. Closing his eyes, he reared up and over, lying on his back. He felt her shift next to him, felt her move up snug to his side in the dark of the tent. He slung an arm over his eyes so he wouldn't have to see her beautiful face, but it didn't matter.

She was imprinted in his thoughts; images of her he'd never forget. Katy trudging determinedly up the mountain, refusing to give up. Wet and slick from the lake water, splashing him full in the face and laughing out loud, as she so rarely did. Katy, standing in the river, her perfect, luscious body taunting him, as did her eyes.

He loved her. Desperately, helplessly. But to give in, then watch her leave when it was over, would kill him.

He felt her lean over him, pull his arm from his face,

and when her lips brushed his jaw, his every muscle tightened in defense. "Don't do this," he begged her even as her lips slid down over his throat.

"Yes," she whispered.

"It's not me you want," he managed, even though she'd planted her wet, warm open mouth at the base of his neck. His hands fisted at his sides, bunching and unbunching in the sleeping bag beneath him.

"It's you," she promised.

Because he couldn't help himself, he touched her arms, ran his palms slowly up and down over them. "You're trying to dispel the dream. There are other ways—"

His words were lost when she reared up and took his mouth. When she came up for air, her eyes were glittery. "You're nervous. It's sweet."

"You're crazy."

"Yeah, maybe." But she kissed him again, a deep, drugging kiss that nearly stole the last of his resolve. Nearly. The T-shirt she wore glimmered in the night, white, virgin, completely without frills. Her long, creamy limbs wrapped around him.

With damp hands, he tried to set her away from him, and ended up gripping her tight. "This is a mistake."

"Very likely," she agreed, her busy mouth attacking his ear.

If he hadn't been lying down, he would have slid bonelessly to the floor. If ever he'd seen a more beautiful, desirable woman, he couldn't remember. And never had he wanted a woman so intensely, so sharply that it was a physical pain.

But it scared him, this unreasonable fear he had that

she would run hard and fast the minute this was over. "I'm not going to touch you," he told her shakily even as his palms continued over her arms and down the perfect curve of her back. "Not like this. Not here."

"No problem," she told him, her own voice wavering a little. "I'll touch you."

God, no. If she did, he'd be lost. But she evaded his efforts to catch her hands, and she tugged on the string that held up his sweats. Her hands were steadier than his as she streaked them up and over his chest again while he gripped her hips to hold her away from him.

She simply pressed harder, until those hips rocked over his. He couldn't stifle his moan, or the need that swelled over him at her movements.

"So strong," she whispered. "So hard."

Her lips were soft and coaxing, and pressed against him as she was, he could feel her heart pounding. His entire body tensed, and several times he started to reach for her automatically before he caught himself. "No," he said thickly even as his mouth clung to hers. "This isn't what you really want."

But her lips trailed again over his jaw as her fingers toyed with the waistband of his sweats. "Right this minute I want you, Kyle."

"For this minute, yes," he rasped out when her teeth nibbled on his ear. "But not forever."

"Forever has nothing to do with this. Love me, Kyle. Please, make love to me."

To stop this madness, he put his hands on her shoulders. "No. You're awake now. And . . . fine." She was more than fine, she was beyond his wildest dreams. "I'll go. Before it's too late."

"It's already too late," she murmured. In the darkness her eyes shimmered at him. "You've done something to me. Showed me more than I've ever hoped for. Let me show you something back, Kyle."

Still, he might have resisted. But her questing fingers slid beneath his sweats and encircled the desperate, leaping, hot part of him that would have begged her for possession. "God, Katy."

He had no idea if he was praying for mercy, or for more of what she was giving him. Probably both. She gave it, and he could only moan. The last teensy-weensy part of his brain that was functioning properly realized that she was the only woman for him, and that he should take whatever part of her she would give. But still, he held back.

"Please," she whispered. "I want to love you." Then she shoved impatiently at his sweats, freeing him to the cool night and her hot gaze. She stroked him, and he thought he would die of pleasure, of pain. "I want to love you," she whispered again, then replaced her hands with her mouth.

Though he wished she meant more than the physical, he could hardly think, much less breathe. Her sweet, hot breath, her tongue . . . But because he knew she meant only this, that she only wanted to love him this way, his capitulation was made all the more bittersweet.

Pulling her up and away from him was another sort of torture. "And I want to love you," he said, giving in to the urgency that threatened to drown them both. When he tugged her down on top of him, he scored his hot, eager mouth over her neck, her jaw, her face. Then he met her lips with his own and showed her all the heat, all the pent-up passion he'd been holding back.

Reaching down between them, she touched him again, and he moaned into her mouth. It was so easy to let it overcome him, to let the fire and raging desire take them both. Rolling over in the small tent, they became an entangled mass of limbs. Thick down covered her from him, and impatiently he tore away the sleeping bag to cover her with himself. The thin cotton she wore was more an enticement than a barrier. Fascinated by her smooth, white skin, he feasted as the shirt rose high on her thigh. When he slipped his hands beneath the shirt, skimming over her flat belly, her ribs, around to her slim back, she whispered his name in a low, needy whimper, arousing them both.

Scrunching up the material, exposing her to his gaze, he drank his fill. Her nipples hardened instantly, and though she wore bikini panties, he would have sworn he could see the heat between her legs. Her body stretched out before him in all its toned, willowy glory. Never had he seen anything more beautiful, and he told her so.

"Kyle," she whispered. "Touch me."

He did, letting his hands roam as he pleased. He'd wanted to touch her for so long, he wasn't about to rush. He loved the texture of her skin, how dark his own looked next to hers in the pale moonlight. Fingertips teased and grazed her breasts until she moved restlessly beneath him. Then he took her hardened nipple into his mouth, and she cried out.

"Shhh." He slipped his fingers beneath the edge of her panties and found the wet, slippery center of her, rising up to swallow her cry.

His hands shook as he removed her clothes and he realized something shocking. *Never* had anything meant so much. He'd make damn sure she felt the same way, even if it killed him. And judging by the size of his erection, it just might.

Wanting to pleasure her, even knowing it would only hurt all the more when she left him, he rose up on his knees and shoved off his sweats. Bending over her, he kissed her neck, suckled at her breasts, and his blood heated as she panted and clung to him. Kissing a path over her belly, he tongued his way between her legs. At his first taste, they both moaned.

Her hands fisted tightly, painfully, in his hair, but he didn't care. He hardly felt it, compared with the pain of his arousal. Working her into a frenzy beneath him with his tongue and fingers, he smiled when she shuddered and begged for more. When her muscles went limp, he climbed up her body with his mouth leading the way as his hands spread her thighs. He'd give her what she was sobbing for, and even if they never made love again, she'd not forget this time.

He parted her mouth with his tongue and made love to it as he thrust himself into her. Arching her hips, her head thrown back, she gasped, and took him into her eagerly. She squeezed him close as he filled her, driving deep and retreating in a rhythm as old as time.

"More," she whispered. "More, Kyle." And she raised her hips to meet his every thrust. He lifted her thighs so he could go more deeply inside her. They both sighed harshly when he did. They took each other fast and hard, their hearts racing to the same beat. Emotion mingled with passion. Fear of the future faded to the heat of the moment.

Her eyes opened, filled with a dark intensity and more emotion than he could have hoped for. A lump lodged in his throat at the incredible sweetness of it all. "I love you," he said thickly, unable to hold the words back. Her instant climax ripped through them both. He hovered for a flash on the brink of ecstasy, but his own release pounded through him, and he clung to her as if he were a dying man.

Eventually, she relaxed beneath him, sighing long and soft. Her chest rose and fell softly, her damp skin still clinging to his.

He stared down at her in wonder, his soul stripped bare, thoroughly shaken by the forces they'd shared. Another soft breath reached him, and he blinked the darkness away. Then had to laugh at himself.

Apparently, the counselor hadn't been nearly so shaken, or destroyed.

She'd fallen fast asleep.

When Kyle woke up a short time later, he shivered. The cool night air blew in from beneath the flap of the tent, dusting over their bare skin. He covered their chilled bodies with Katherine's sleeping bag, which was bunched at their feet.

As he raised up she murmured a protest and clung tightly to his chest. Smiling, he settled back down and snuggled her close.

"I'm not leaving," he whispered, but she slept on. It should have pleased him, how utterly comfortable she was with him. And it did. He could lie there in a tangled heap of warmth with her forever. But her unnaturally deep sleep told him she hadn't slept in far too long. So did the faint shadows beneath her eyes.

Holding her as tightly as he could without waking her, he kissed her gently. "Sleep all you want, baby, I'm not going anywhere."

In slumber, she sighed.

ELEVEN

Before dawn, Katherine blinked . . . and froze. Her face was plastered to a bare chest—a bare, hard, warm, sexy one. Her arms were wrapped around the waist beneath that chest, and long, sinewy arms encased her as well, holding her close enough so she could feel his heart beating strong and even. Powerful, lean, masculine legs were entwined with hers, one of them even resting intimately between hers, high enough to be rubbing against her— oh, God.

She was nude and so was he.

She groaned as it all came back to her; her nightmare, Kyle racing to her tent to comfort her, her seducing him. *Oh, God.*

It was the truth, *she'd* seduced *him. She'd* stayed with *him* after. *She'd* slept against *him* like a baby in her crib. Which gave her no one to blame but herself. She hated that.

But he felt so good wrapped around her. If there was a better-looking, more magnificently made male, she hadn't seen him. His face was relaxed in sleep. His mouth . . . God, that mouth. Even now she longed to have it smile lazily, then kiss her. She had no idea anyone could kiss as he'd kissed her. Soul-destroying, heart-melting kisses that lasted for days, each one chipping away at her composure until she was a whimpering mass of jelly.

He was something. Long, tanned limbs, filled with sinewy, corded strength. Sleek chest, tight belly, powerful legs . . . There wasn't an extra ounce of fat on his body, anywhere.

Oh, he was something, all right. But he wasn't hers. Not now, not ever. He couldn't be.

The California Cowboy and the Prosecuting Attorney. Didn't fit, never would. His world was too . . . What was it? Right now all she could think was that it seemed pretty darn perfect.

Too perfect. Panic overwhelmed her.

Sleepy brown eyes opened, and he smiled at her. "Hey," he said softly, leaning in for the kiss she'd wished for just a second earlier.

He must have felt her resistance, for he frowned and lifted his head. "What's the matter—" He broke off to swear, then his arms tightened on her. "You're regretting this already, damn you."

"I don't know what I'm doing." Her voice sounded a little hysterical, even to her own ears. "I'm sorry—"

He rolled back and sighed. "Oh, great," he said to the ceiling of the tent. "It's the 'I'm-sorry routine.' "

"Kyle—"

"Don't." His voice was low, husky, and unbearably arousing. "Please, don't say anything else. I have a great aversion to sleeping with you when you're playing the attorney."

"Fine." Cloaking herself in icy disdain was an old habit and would protect her from the hurt. "But since I *am* an attorney, I guess you'll have to leave."

It was too dark still to see his expression as he wordlessly rose and jerked on his sweats, but she was fairly certain it wasn't filled with the tender passion that had been there only a moment before.

She bit back the protest and the hurt in her heart and let him go.

Though the sun hadn't yet peeked above the mountain, Kyle stalked to the river, shrugging into the shirt he'd grabbed. The air was a little crisp, but not cold.

Yet it was strange how fast he could feel chilled to the bone. He'd lain there next to the sweetest, warmest female he'd ever known, and grown cold as ice.

He'd hoped for too much from her, he'd dreamed too hard and fast that she could overcome her fear of emotion. He'd fooled himself.

He was an idiot.

An idiot who heard her coming, making her way through the brush.

"You left in a hurry," she whispered into the breaking dawn, standing behind him.

"At your invitation."

From somewhere in a distance, an owl hooted. There was an answering call. The wind blew over them, rippling the already swift water.

"I'm not very good in these sorts of situations," she said uneasily.

"How about 'thanks for the great lay, see you around sometime'?" he suggested lightly, though his stomach clenched hard and uncomfortably.

"I didn't mean to cast you aside like you were in my way," she said softly. "And I certainly didn't mean to make you feel like you were just one in a line of many."

"Apparently it's too late for that," he murmured, watching the water rush over the rocks. "Because I do feel that way." He fought back humiliation as he remembered the emotions she caused in him. *Still caused.* "But that's my problem, not yours."

She stepped up beside him, covered from head to toe in stretch pants and that T-shirt of hers, looking rumpled, tousled, and far more stunningly beautiful than she had a right to look. Just watching her hurt. "You're not in my way," she said. "And you're—well, it'd been a long time for me."

He didn't know what to say.

A disparaging sound escaped her. "Kyle, what is it you want from me?"

"At the moment some peace and quiet." He kicked at a rock and crossed his arms so she wouldn't see his trembling hands. "I enjoy watching the sunrise alone."

"You're trying to make me feel guilty, and I don't have anything to feel guilty about."

"No, you don't," he told her, watching the first glimmer of sunlight shimmer off the water. "Go back to bed, Counselor."

"I—oh, hell." Her head slumped between her shoulders and for a long moment she studied her booted feet.

She swiped at a strand of blond hair, watched the trees as they blew and swayed high above them. "I threw myself at you."

Unwillingly, a grin tugged at his lips. "Yes, and I fought you like mad, but you won."

"This isn't very funny, Kyle."

"Gotta get your laughs where you can. Better run, Katherine. You might get the urge to jump my bones again."

Her lips twisted wryly. "I deserved that, I suppose. Both the comment and the use of my full name." She sighed. "Sick thing is," she whispered, "I do have that urge. To jump you, that is."

His head whipped up to look at her. "No." But he grinned in spite of himself. "This time I mean it."

She'd moved close, wrapped her arms around his middle, and planted her face to his chest. His hands moved to her shoulders, to push her away, to pull her close—he had no idea which. "Katy, this isn't the answer."

Going up on tiptoe, she brushed her lips over his jaw. "I'm sorry I hurt you, Kyle. Last night *did* mean something to me. It *was* special."

"Katy—"

She silenced him with her lips. "I want you," she whispered, dragging her lips over his lightly stubbled face to nibble on his ear. "Too much, but I do. Please, say it's enough."

He wanted to say a whole hell of a lot of things. Wanted to demand to know why being close to someone scared her, but she'd deny that. He wanted to tell her again how he felt, and make her deal with it, but that would be useless. The counselor would deal with nothing before she was ready.

In the end he said nothing, but grabbed her and swung her up against him, heading deeper into the woods. Laughing breathlessly, she clung to him, meeting his intense, dark gaze.

"This isn't even close to over," he told her as he set her down before a giant sequoia in a heavily wooded area. "And I'm going to prove it to you once and for all."

Eyes lit with excitement, hunger, and a trace of fear, she reached for him as he backed her hard to the tree. "Show me."

What happened next was like the second storm of the night before; blinding hunger, intense need, unbearable heat. Before Katherine could draw a ragged breath, he had her pants off and his sweats open. Lifting her off the ground, he impaled her.

His voice sounded like gravel. "Lift your legs, baby. Like that." One stroke and she came violently, shuddering around him. Another, and he was right behind her.

"Oh, my God," she breathed against his neck. "Oh, my God."

He was trembling so badly, he was afraid he'd drop her. Letting her legs slide down his body, he leaned on her, against the tree. "Are you okay?"

The sun came up around them. Her eyes fluttered open and she gazed solemnly at him, the flush of arousal still on her face. "What have you done to me?"

He let out a little smile. "Nearly killed you, I think. Myself too." Bending, he picked up her pants and helped her into them, then righted his own clothes.

"I . . . don't know how to deal with this." She

sounded bewildered, confused, and it made him want to hold her again, but she held him off. "I need to think, Kyle. I can't do that with you touching me. I can't even do that with you looking at me." She laughed, shakily. "Who am I kidding? I can't even *look* at you and think. I don't get it."

"Don't you?" he murmured. His legs were still shaking. So was his soul.

"No. We come from two different worlds, Kyle," she said, apology thick in her voice. "How can we make something like this work?"

"The way you make anything work." He shrugged, but his heart twisted a little. "You just have to want it badly enough."

"I really didn't want to want this," she said softly, raising terror-filled eyes to his.

"If only it were so simple." And if only he didn't care so very much.

"It is simple."

"Nothing's simple when it comes to the heart," he said.

She looked at him for one more minute, then suddenly covered her face with her hands. "You're right," she said, her voice muffled. "It's difficult. So damned difficult."

He wondered if she had any idea how scared she really was of him and what he made her feel, if she realized how she hid behind this different-world thing. But she swallowed hard, torment blazing from her eyes. Yes she does, he thought. She knows and it doesn't change a thing.

Patience. Time. She needed both.

He opened his arms, relieved when she walked into

them. "Don't worry about it, Katy. Not now. It'll work out."

She squeezed him close. Over her head he watched the sun light up everything around him and tried to convince himself that he spoke the truth. It would work out. It would.

Please, let it work out.

For two more glorious days they rode the river. They passed miles and miles of walls that rose two hundred feet to the sky, saw side-canyon waterfalls, prehistoric rock art, and deep, cavern caves. The vivid contrast between utter tranquillity and the all-out adventure of the rapids was a thrill.

Kyle was busy, very busy, keeping the four of them afloat, keeping the raft in one piece, and scouting out places to stop each night.

At the end of the river journey, when they'd been on the trek for a total of two weeks, Katherine sat and watched the sunrise.

Alone.

She'd climbed out of her tent, her heart tripping a little in anticipation of watching Kyle watch the morning. She loved to watch him.

But she'd been alone, no Kyle in sight.

He'd been careful to give her space, yet make sure that she was never alone. He'd laughed and joked with Chris and Bettina, told her stories of his journeys, and made sure that the raft ride was something she'd never forget. Each night he'd set up his tent as close as possible to hers, but hadn't tried so much as to kiss her.

Which, she reminded herself, was exactly as she wanted it.

So why did she feel so unbearably lonely?

As the sun rose up and over the lovely meadow in which they'd camped, lighting up each dew-covered rock, each individual blade of grass, each treetop, the truth slammed home.

She loved it out here.

In a little less than a week she'd be back at home, behind a desk, pushing around files. She'd be in a brick building from sunup to sundown, without once experiencing a fresh, cool breeze or the distant hoot of an owl.

It hurt. But what hurt even more was that she would no longer have an excuse to exercise what had become her favorite pastime.

Kyle-watching.

For two days she'd done little else. He really believed in what he was doing, and his love and passion for the outdoors showed in his every move. Maybe that was good, that he wasn't exposed to the harsh reality of the everyday world that was her life. She couldn't imagine him being happy anywhere other than on a mountaintop.

In just two weeks he'd come to mean so much to her, so much more than she would have thought possible. But she didn't have the words to tell him that, and even if she had, she wouldn't have spoken them. She would go back to her life, and he to his. And yes, there would be pain, *so* much pain. But there was no reason to drag out what could never be.

"Good morning."

At the sound of the low, husky voice she'd come to know so well, she jumped nervously. Unsmiling, eyes dark with an intensity she didn't understand, he sat down on the log beside her and turned his gaze to the beautiful morning.

"You missed most of it," she said. Her voice came quick, light, and whispery. Already, she was out of breath, as if she'd been running miles uphill.

The knowing look he turned on her had her flushing. "I overslept."

"Overslept? You never—" She stopped, suddenly understanding. He'd been keeping a vigil on her at night. With all the work he did during the day, she could only imagine how tired he must be. "Kyle, you don't have to do this."

He reached for her hand, rubbed his fingers over her knuckles. "You sleeping better?"

"Yes. Thanks to you."

"Thanks to my phone, you mean." His lips quirked and he shook his head. "Ready to make your call?"

They'd called her office together every morning, just to check in. So far she'd managed to miss Ted, but Stacey had been keeping her informed. It seemed that she was out of danger since the senator had told Ted that his son had left for their Switzerland chalet to hide out for a while. Which meant that in just one week, when this trek was over, she'd be fine.

Just fine, she repeated to herself, when her heart sent up a little protest. "It's probably not necessary to call today," she told Kyle. "Since we know everything's okay."

He frowned. "Call anyway."

His protectiveness was like a balm. She glanced down at his hand covering hers. It was work-roughened, big and warm. His fingers were long, his nails trimmed short. She remembered exactly what those fingers could do to her, and she blushed again—with arousal. The image of those hands gripping her hips tight as he—

"You okay?"

"Fine," she said faintly, feeling her cheeks flare with heat. She just managed to meet his curious stare. His tongue came out to lick at his slightly chapped lips. An image of that tongue darting out to slather warmly over her—

"Are you sure?" he questioned, leaning in close. "You look a little flushed."

She laughed weakly. "Oh, Kyle. I think you'd better go. You're in danger here."

His brows came together sharply as he looked around. But understanding dawned as he jerked his head back to her. Quietly, slowly, his light brown eyes took in her reddened face, lingering at her lips. Then they went on a slow perusal of her body. His eyes blazed hotly. Silly as it seemed, she'd never felt so attractive in all her life.

"I've missed you," she whispered, squeezing his hand.

"Can we establish that we're talking about a physical sort of 'miss,' and not a mental thing?" he asked quietly.

Oh, it was definitely physical, but the scariest part of all was that it was so much more. She couldn't admit that, could she? She let a grin curve her lips. "Is there something wrong with a bad case of lust, Kyle?"

"Definitely not."

"Well, then," she murmured, reaching for him.

He held her off, his hands gripping her upper arms. Hunger and need erupted through him like a geyser at what she was offering. "Not this time."

"Not this time?" she repeated in surprise.

"I don't mix pleasure with business."

Her mouth opened. Then closed. "You did once before. *Twice*, actually."

At the memory of that unforgettable night and morning, his arousal strained behind his zipper. He'd never look at a giant sequoia quite the same way again. "That was different."

"How?"

"I thought—" *Dammit.* How could she not see this? Had he gotten nowhere with this woman? Had nothing he said made any sense at all? "I love you, Katy."

She flinched, which only fueled him on. "I want you to be happy. And safe, free from fear and terror. There's so much I want for you. But I have to have it back. You have to give something back, or it's no good."

She'd gone pale beneath her light tan. Her eyes looked huge in her face. "I missed you, Kyle," she whispered, her expression taut with the rejection she'd thought he'd just served her. "I don't understand any of this, but that's one thing that remains clear. I'd hoped that would be enough."

And he was supposed to resist her? "You care for me," he said carefully.

She looked at him, her wide gray eyes swirling with emotions, matching the light mist that covered the meadow.

"Why is that so hard to admit?" he wanted to know.

"Why do we have to complicate this?"

His shoulders drooped. He stood more abruptly than he'd intended, and she nearly fell off the log. "I'm sorry," he told her, sorrow washing through his veins. "I have to get breakfast going."

Her lips tightened. Her eyes closed. "I guess this means there will be no mixing pleasure and business this morning."

"Save your energy, Counselor." He turned away and walked toward the bikes. "You're going to need it."

TWELVE

On her first bike ride in years, Katherine bit back her nerves.

Everyone was watching her with mixed expressions. Chris was amused because she'd refused to admit that maybe she needed advice. Bettina was worried, clucking like a mother hen, constantly remembering something new Katherine would need to know.

But Kyle's expression was by far the most complex. Everything she'd hoped for, and everything she feared most, was there, and she couldn't easily face it.

Head down, she studied the bike beneath her. "Doesn't seem so tough."

Chris laughed. "You might not be saying that in eight hours."

Katherine closed her eyes for a minute and tried not to think about how long eight hours on a tiny, hard seat was. And how her bottom was going to take it. "No problem."

Kyle came close on his bike, saying nothing. In fact,

he'd said very little to her since their last discussion, which had gone nowhere. She knew he was hurt and trying not to show it so she wouldn't feel any worse.

But she hurt too. The thought that in a few short days she'd be back in the city, far away from him, had her stomach clenching.

Then she glanced down the rock bowl they'd be riding and her stomach stayed clenched, nervously.

His bike stopped right next to hers. She looked at him and promptly forgot her fear. He stood, straddling the bike, his shoulders wide and taut in his tight shirt, his arms flexed. His legs were exposed by his biker shorts, two long, lean, powerful lengths of pure muscle. Her mouth watered, then went dry.

How could such undiluted lust seize her now, when she was poised at the top of a huge granite basin, getting ready to kill herself on a bike?

With a light touch, he reached over both bikes and tightened her helmet, staring deep into her eyes the entire time.

He smiled that soft, knowing smile, as if he knew exactly what he did to her and liked it. "Remember to sit loosely in the seat. Don't tense. This first part is sandy. Whatever you do, don't stop abruptly. Try to glide through any problem spots."

"Right." She tried not to snicker. "Just glide on through."

"You know how to do that real well, Counselor. You'll be fine."

His slight sarcastic tone gave her the push of adrenaline she needed, and she *was* fine. Deliciously, deliriously so.

Riding was like no experience in her life, and she loved it. The solitude, the unparalleled beauty, and the challenging bike terrain exhilarated her. So did the sheer vertical uplifts they rode beneath, the plunging gorges . . . it was all part of a landscape she knew she'd never forget.

They passed a faintly detectable, narrow road, one that Kyle told them was an old wagon road first carved into the mountain by immigrants one hundred and fifty years before.

Several hours after lunch, steeped in all the compliments everyone had given her, they came to a particularly steep trail down.

Bettina and Chris, as they loved to do, went for it, screeching and hooting the entire way.

Kyle laughed and turned to Katherine. "I don't want you to do that," he said. "Zigzag down. Take it slow."

"Why?" She met his gaze. "Think I can't do it?"

"I think you can do anything you want to," he said carefully, slowly.

"But not this."

Again, he hesitated. "I'm not trying to tell you what to do here, Katherine, but—"

So they were back to Katherine, were they? "I'll have you know, this ride has been a piece of cake."

Now he bit his cheek. His eyes lit with what she could only hope wasn't humor, though she suspected it was. *He was laughing at her.* "Look—"

"See you at the bottom," she quipped as she pushed off and prayed.

For the first few terrifying seconds as she headed

straight down the rocky trail, she heard him right behind her. "Go away," she called out to him. "I'm—"

Turning her head back forward, she had time to open her mouth before she smashed into the tree.

As she lay there in an unhurt tangled heap of her own limbs and bike, the irony of the whole thing hit her. She'd acted as rotten as a nightmarish defense attorney.

"Katy. God, Katy." In a flash Kyle was beside her, holding her down when she would have risen up. "No, hold still."

"I'm not hurt," she told him wryly. "At least not physically."

Obviously, he didn't believe her. Strong, capable hands ran over her carefully and so thoroughly, whatever breath she'd managed to preserve backed up in her throat. Still, he wasn't satisfied. His fingers ran back up her legs, gently squeezing the entire length. When he got to the top of her thighs, his fingers brushed the core of her. Not noticing, still wearing a tight frown, he continued back over her stomach, up her ribs. Her breasts tightened painfully.

He didn't even glance at them. When he finally ran his hands down her arms one last time, she let out her breath slowly through her teeth. "Satisfied?"

Gently, he squeezed her waist and peered at her anxiously. "Nothing hurts?"

What hurt was the strange, swirling sensation in her breasts and between her legs, and how he hadn't even noticed during his impersonal search. "I'm not sure," she said with a weak smile, lying back. "Better check me again, Doc."

He stared at her, then his shoulders slumped in relief.

"I can't believe you. You went headlong into that tree—you took ten years off my life. *Twenty*."

"You just gave me at least ten," she joked faintly. Her body tingled, then tingled some more.

For the first time he seemed to realize what she meant. A reluctant smile touched his lips. "Very funny. You gave me a heart attack and you want to discuss sex."

Gingerly, she sat up. She didn't have a scratch on her. "Who said anything about discussing?"

His jaw tightened, his eyes heated. "You blasted yourself into that tree because you got too cocky."

She opened her mouth to object, but he glared at her, making her remain silent. Hands on his hips, kneeling in the dirt, he said tightly, "I'm supposed to be in charge here, Counselor. That means *I* set the rules. You just about killed yourself because you didn't listen, and I won't have it. Are you even listening now?"

She'd turned from him and he whipped her back around. "Now you want to treat what we had like a joke. As if it were a hot little one-nighter."

Had? What they had? As in past tense? That was what she wanted, but she hadn't expected the slash of agony at the realization. She swallowed at the immense pain in his eyes, at the absolute fury and banked temper she'd never suspected. "Kyle, I—"

"Be quiet, Katy. What we had was hot, yes, but it wasn't just a quickie thing for me. Play it as you will, but stop referring to it that way. It bugs the hell out of me."

"I'm sorry," she said quietly, stunned by his words, the amount of hurt she'd caused.

"Keep it up, and—"

"And what?" she asked softly, meeting his angry eyes.

He shook his head. "I'm just in the mood to take you on." But he rose and pulled her up. "Never mind."

"Kyle—" What? What could she say? Don't be angry that she couldn't give him what he thought he wanted from her? That she could never be the sort of woman he needed?

He waited, but she still didn't know what to say. *Don't be hurt*, she wanted to cry. But it was far too late for that.

They were five miles into the second day's bike ride, and Katherine was loving it. Chris and Bettina were in front, single file, and Kyle behind her as they rode along the granite basin of a great long ridge.

It was incredible.

Almost incredible enough to make Katherine forget how she'd hurt Kyle. How she'd hurt herself.

Life is too short, a little voice told her. *What would it hurt to go for it? To give him the chance he's asking for? How much more hurt can you stand?*

She hadn't realized she'd stopped until Kyle got off his bike and came toward her, pulling off his helmet. "Katy?"

At least he still called her Katy. Through her misty vision, she gave him a watery smile. "I'm fine."

She didn't sound fine and he frowned, pulling off her helmet. " 'Fine,' huh?"

She nodded, and he shook his head. "Back to that, are we?"

"Let it go," she whispered, sniffing. "Please."

All around them, rock and granite were spread out in formations older than she could imagine. The sky stretched before them, painfully clear and bright. A lone bird flew overhead.

It was so beautiful, so perfectly beautiful. So was the man standing before her, watching her quietly, worriedly.

"I've been riding behind you," he said in a low voice. "Thinking how proud I am of you. You've done so good, Katy, come so far. Do you realize it?"

She gave him a little smile. For a minute, she thought, dropping her forehead to his chest, just for a minute she'd let him be the strong one. She felt his lips softly at her temple, his hands run through her hair. "It'll be strange to go back," she whispered.

He shrugged, and the muscles of his chest contracted, his wide shoulders lifted. "So don't."

She laughed to hide the pain. "You know I have to."

"All I know is that you could do whatever you want." He touched her face. "But if you do go back, are you going to let me visit you?"

"I will go back," she said firmly, though her heart leaped at what he was asking. "I have to." But she smiled a little. "It might be nice to see you."

His eyes lit with the things she wasn't ready to face, so she turned from him. He turned her back, wrapped his arms around her, and put his lips to hers.

It was new, being kissed this way by him, softly, quietly, as if they had forever to give in to what was happening. His mouth coaxed responses from her that were terrifying. Breathlessly, she lifted her head. "We have to go."

"In a minute," he told her, and kissed her again. He could kiss her all day and never get enough. He soaked up her startled murmur, the way she leaned against him as if she were weak. He wondered if she realized how much she told him in each sweet, little kiss. Her soft sigh filled his mouth, and still he kissed her.

She clung to him, but in a different way than before. It wasn't the unbearable heat drawing them together, it wasn't driving passion that existed between them so strongly, but a more thrilling and very unmistakable emotion.

Love. She loved him.

She murmured with pleasure, with soft acquiescence, and offered him more, opened up and gave him everything she had.

He reveled in that, and in the way she arched against him, rubbing her hips over his.

"Ah, Katy," he murmured, working his way over her jaw to her ear. His hand worked its way down over her tight, curved bottom, so perfectly outlined in her biking shorts. "You feel so good. Will you feel this good in the city with your suits and stockings?"

She stiffened a little, and he knew regret that he'd brought too much reality into their embrace. Patience, he reminded himself a little too late. She'd required buckets of it.

Pulling back, she gave him a cool smile. "I might be pretty busy," she said offhandedly, regaining her composure with annoying ease.

Knowing he would chase her away the harder he pushed, he backed off. "Of course you will." He handed her the helmet he'd removed before, then fastened it for her. "We all have a life, Katy."

Which, given the stunned look her face had taken on, gave her plenty of food for thought.

"You haven't asked much about mine," he said carefully. "My life, that is."

He watched her expression close up right before his eyes. "Why is that?"

"I don't like to pry."

"There's that prissy attorney tone again," he chided mildly. "And you like to pry plenty. I heard you ask Chris and Bettina at least a thousand questions about their personal lives."

"Their jobs are fascinating."

He nodded. "And mine is not."

"It's not that." She made a sound, half frustration, half annoyance. "I think what you do is very exciting."

"But . . . ?" He smiled a little grimly. "I think I hear one at the end of that statement."

"But—" She broke off. Her eyes filled with immeasurable sorrow. "But I feel something for you, Kyle. Something I don't understand. We come from different worlds."

"It's hard to understand how you could say that," he said quietly, "when you have no idea what world I come from." His fault, he thought. He could have told her. He could tell her now. But he wouldn't. Not until she accepted him this way.

She said nothing more.

"I feel something for you too," he told her evenly. "I feel a lot."

"You've said." Her breath hitched.

"I've said twice now." His voice wasn't altogether

steady either. "And both times you've treated it as though I was talking about the weather."

"It's not an easy thing for me to discuss." Her eyes clouded. "I didn't expect you to . . ."

"Fall in love with you? Is that what you're finding so difficult to say?" Now he practically growled in frustration. "Well, I can hardly wait to see how you react when I tell you I can't see the rest of my life without you in it."

She blanched and he had to laugh, though it hurt like hell. "Maybe the idea will grow on you."

Katherine stood rooted to the spot, unable to do anything but stare at him. "But . . ."

"But what?" Taking a chance, he snagged her hips again, drew her stiff body close.

Her shoulders lifted. "I don't know." To his relief, she rested her head on his shoulder and he gave in to the urge to run his hands down her slim back. "I told you once before I can't think when you touch me," she whispered. "Well, now I don't even know my own name."

He did laugh then. And despite her doomsayer expression, his heart lifted. She would get used to it. She had no choice. For she did love him. More than she knew.

Ah, he could see them now. Leaning out of the tree he'd climbed, he peered through the binoculars. The sharpshooter rifle he'd brought leaned comfortably against his leg on the branch on which he sat.

In another few minutes they'd ride directly beneath him, and Katherine Wilson would be history. So, out of spite, would the trekkers she traveled with. They'd certainly caused him enough trouble over the past two weeks, trying to track them all down.

Ridiculous. A man of his stature shouldn't be forced to go through this. Camping, for God's sake. But they'd pay. All of them.

And in the end he'd win. He'd be the next senator. Then from here, president. His possibilities were endless.

All he had to do was get rid of the woman whom people were beginning to like better than him. Grinning, he reached for the gun and waited.

She rode in the back, though Kyle checked on her often. Katherine smiled at him and waved, letting him know she was fine.

Chris and Bettina wanted to career down this last bowl for the pure thrill of it, and she knew Kyle did too. She didn't want to hold them back, but she wasn't about to bonsai down that steep, rocky hill. No, since her head-long introduction to that tree, she felt much more comfortable with her speed—a slow crawl.

She was having more fun than she would have believed. There was just something about having the wind whip her hair from her face, having the sun warm her skin, having the quick, hard tremor of excitement over-come her as she rode down over the rocks into the bottom of the basin.

Plus, she felt wonderfully safe. At lunch, Kyle had made her again call the office. Ted hadn't been there, but Stacey had patched her through to him on his mobile phone. He'd sounded a little breathless, a little surprised to hear from her, but he'd assured her she was safe. The press exposure had died down, and the senator still had his son out of the country.

Pausing halfway down the bowl, she stood straddling her bike, her breath coming in excited pants. Towering trees shaded her from the sun, so she had a clear view of the steep descent of Chris, Bettina, and Kyle as they raced to the bottom, whooping and hollering.

Kyle was the loudest, and his joy at the unbounded freedom of the ride was contagious.

Their voices echoed in the canyon, and Katherine found herself laughing at them. She wished she could keep up. Maybe next year.

Maybe next year?

Oh, she was far gone to have let that thought escape, and she shuffled it to the back of her mind. Putting her feet back into the stirrups of her bike, she prepared to continue her slow, careful ride down.

When the shot sounded, she jerked in surprise and shock, and promptly fell off her bike. Because of the steep incline along which she'd been riding, she slid down the mountain, grappling in vain for a grip, cutting her hands and knees.

This time there was no tree in her path to stop her descent, and she slid uncontrollably.

Above her, two more shots sounded, then came a sound that had her skin crawling and fear racing up her spine.

It was a laugh.

Finally, skidding to a halt in the dirt and rocks, she lifted her head, her heart in her throat. From her low vantage point, she could no longer see the three bikes below her. Trees and thick brush blocked her vision, even when she stretched desperately. Her stomach knotted.

Had the shots been directed at them? Oh, God. Where were they? Lifting up on her hands and knees, she froze at the voice coming from directly above her.

"Don't move. You're next."

THIRTEEN

Ignoring the order, Katherine lifted her head and stared up into the tree above her. Ted's tight mouth twisted into a leer, and he waved with the hand that wasn't on his gun.

Her vision wavered, but she could see that his frown grew more ferocious. "Don't you dare pass out," he gritted out. "Not until you know exactly what's going to happen to you."

"Ted?" Disbelief made her shake her head, thinking she was hallucinating. Please, let this all be another nightmare.

"Who else? Mohany, maybe?" He laughed and Katherine blanched.

"It's . . . been you this entire time?"

"My, you're quick." He shook his head. "Did you know you've been named Woman of the Year? Of course, you didn't. You've been on vacation these past two weeks. At the luncheon they're having for you next month, they're going to ask you to consider running for office."

"Office?" No, this wasn't happening. Kyle wasn't

dead. She wasn't on a mountainside, bleeding, having a calm discussion with her boss.

"After your stint as DA, naturally." His mouth twisted cruelly. "Seems they like you better than me. And I had such high hopes for myself," he added calmly. "Still do. Especially now that you'll be out of the picture."

"No," she whispered, her eyes darting down the granite basin, searching in vain for any sign of life. *Nothing*. Her knees wobbled. Ruthlessly, she forced herself upright.

"Sorry," he said, shifting on the branch, rising up a little to better aim the gun. "It has to be this way. Mohany was supposed to finish this off for me, but I couldn't trust him." He peered over her where the three bikes had disappeared.

Rage and grief welled up, threatened to overcome her. He'd killed Bettina and Chris. And Kyle. The love of her life. Oh, God. Again, she wavered, but with the strength born of pure resolve, she locked her knees. No. She wouldn't give in to the mourning yet. Not until she saw this through. "You killed them."

"It's not them that interests me." He gestured with the gun. "Come closer."

"No." From her fall on the sharp ground, her knees and hands burned. Still, she backed away. "Why, Ted? Why did they have to die?"

That smile, the full, cheerful, politically correct one she'd admired so many times, made her want to be sick. "I've been following you. You saw me on the river. I even talked to you on the phone. Good thing I had the mobile on me. Stacey was able to patch your call right through.

Of course she had no idea I was actually close enough to talk to you in person."

"I should have guessed . . . you sounded so funny. You've been here the entire time."

"Not at first." His next smile had chills running down her spine. "And don't forget the fox I tossed you."

Bile rose. "You got rid of it fast."

"Had to. Your fearless leader almost caught me." He looked at her over the gun. "Come here."

"No," she whispered.

"Katherine." He lifted the gun and sighted her through the branches. Or tried to. "You're not in a position to argue here."

He'd taken away everything that mattered. He held a gun on her. All she could do was make it as difficult as possible for him. "If you want me closer, you'll have to come get me."

Ted laughed. Sweat trickled down his forehead, dirt lined an arm. She'd never seen him look anything other than perfectly groomed. It made him all the more terrifying.

"Don't tempt me," he said with a growl.

She realized then what was holding him up. From his perch in the tree, and her close angle on the sharp decline beneath him, branches blocked him. He couldn't get a good position, or a good aim at her. "What's the matter, Ted?" She forced a smile as she looked up at him. "Can't do it?"

He scowled and shifted, moving on the branch. She moved, too, back a step, down the mountain a little, and again the branch was in his way.

"Dammit," he cried. "Don't move."

This time when he shifted on the branch, she took two steps back, glancing with longing at the bike on its side. It lay fifteen feet away. That would be of no help to her. But could she slide down far enough to escape him?

Before she had time to wonder, Ted let out a strangled cry and fell from the tree.

Gasping in surprise, Katherine whirled, but before she could start her slide, he'd rolled into her, taking her with him down the sharp decline.

Her shoulder gouged painfully into a rock, her head hit the ground, producing stars in her eyes. Still she pummeled at him as they rolled down, down.

When the gun he still held discharged, she winced in pain, but only because of the noise. With the momentum of both their weights combined, they continued to slide and Katherine reached up for the gun.

Slowly, they came to a stop, and Katherine jerked hard on the gun.

It wasn't necessary.

Ted's eyes were open, but he wasn't moving. Blood gushed from a gash on his forehead, but she still just stared at him. Had he knocked himself out from his fall? Or had she shot him?

Horror filled her so that it took three times before she could free herself of his weight. Even then, she leaned on her hands and knees, shaking violently, panting air into her searing lungs.

Dazed, she lifted her head, hearing for the first time the distant drone of a helicopter. Help was on its way.

A hysterical bubble of laughter worked its way past her chattering teeth. *Help*.

It was far too late for that. She was beyond help,

beyond being able to care that she might need it herself. It didn't matter that she'd started to shiver in spite of the warm sun. Or that her knees and hands bled freely from the fall she'd taken off the bike.

None of that mattered, or would ever matter again.

How could she even think of anything other than what had happened to Chris, Bettina, and Kyle? Thanks to her, three unsuspecting, wonderful, caring people were dead. Including the man of her dreams. *Dead.*

And so was her heart.

She allowed her knocking knees to give out and sank slowly to the ground.

The first shot took Chris, Bettina, and Kyle by surprise. Stupidly, Chris and Bettina stared at each other.

"That couldn't be—" Chris started.

"Not out here," Bettina said, her eyebrows drawing tight together.

Kyle's heart jerked.

"Down!" he shouted. They all dove off their bikes, and he realized they were out of range, too far down the hill.

But Katy was not. The next two shots struck terror through his blood. Lifting his head, he watched her fall off her bike, take a nasty tumble, and slide down the hill.

"Behind the trees," Chris said quickly, yanking both Bettina and Kyle with him.

He went, whipping the mobile phone off his belt as he ran. He called for help as they sprinted for cover, not easy on the steep, rough terrain. He had no idea how long it would take for that help to arrive.

Breathing heavily, the three of them stared at each other, shock and disbelief on each of their faces.

"We can't see from here," Bettina whispered, wringing her hands. "Maybe if we stay in the trees on the edge of the ridge here, we can climb up and see—"

"No," Chris interrupted. "You wait here. Behind the trees. Wait here until help comes. Kyle and I—"

"Stay with her, Chris," Kyle told him. "Wait until you hear the helicopter before you come out. Promise me."

"But—"

"*Promise*," he said quickly, hating each minute that went by while he had no idea what was happening to Katy. "I can't be worried about the two of you and do what I have to do."

Chris stared at him, then nodded slowly, his eyes intent. "We'll wait, then."

Every second seeming like aeons, Kyle slowly worked his way back through the dense trees on the side of the basin. There was no way he would wait for the helicopter.

He had to get to Katy.

As he climbed the sharp incline from which he'd just raced down on his bike, his breath backed up in his throat. His hands were damp, his heart slammed in his chest.

Please, please, let her be unhurt.

He poked his head cautiously up over the last incline, still too far from the clearing in which he'd last seen Katy. But voices came to him, carrying easily on the bare granite basin.

He heard a male voice taunting, telling Katy that she

would be next. That rough voice laughed, and let her think that he'd killed Kyle and the others.

To his shock, Kyle realized Katy believed it. She believed every single word. He hated what he heard in her voice—fear, raw grief, rage—and he climbed the ravine with new haste, not feeling the rocks as they dug into his hands.

When he was able to see over the last ridge, he was only twenty yards from where she stood staring up into a tree. What he saw had his blood freezing in his veins.

As she took a step backward a man tumbled from the tree, directly on top of her. A gun discharged, and both bodies went still.

"No!" he cried even as he charged forward, churning up the rocky terrain between them without effort.

Vaguely he was aware of the helicopter closing in on them, of Bettina and Chris coming up behind him. But all that took a backseat to his mad dash to where Katy lay, trapped beneath a man's body.

Halfway to her, he saw her shove the man off and struggle to her hands and knees. She wavered and put a hand to her head, but she kept her face averted. With her expression hidden from him, and her shoulders slumped, it was impossible to see her clearly and a heavy panic kicked in, followed by an unearthly terror such as he'd never known.

Each breath seared his lungs, but he didn't slow. Wouldn't, until he reached her. If only she'd lift her face, he thought, gasping as he moved. He'd be able to tell how badly hurt she was.

Even though she didn't, he could see she was covered in blood. *Hers?* The man's? God, he couldn't tell, and he was dying a thousand deaths himself wondering as he ran toward her as fast as he could. Then she collapsed.

By the time he reached her side and hit his knees, she was watching him from eyes glazed with shock.

All he could do was grab her and hold her close as the helicopter lowered. Speaking was impossible over the loud roar of the engine as it hovered, searching for a place to land on the uneven, steep ground. Dust, dirt, and rocks flew up, and Kyle, shaken to the core over the unnatural stillness of the woman in his arms, hunched over her, protecting her with his body.

FOURTEEN

Two hours later, when the helicopter had left, risen back up in the air as though it had never landed, the four of them stared at each other. They sat on a series of rocks off to the side of the granite basin, each too shaken to move.

An air of unreality set in.

"I can't believe you didn't take the easy way out and go with the authorities," Bettina said to Katherine. "I probably would have."

"No, you wouldn't," Chris said. "And we're proud that you didn't either, Katherine."

She wasn't hurt, not really. Most of the blood had been from Ted's head injury. He'd bled like a stuck pig. Her knees and hands had been easily swiped clean. Yes, she could have gone with the helicopter—and never seen Kyle again.

It had been pure selfishness that had made her stay for this last ride. After tomorrow, when they arrived back at base camp, she'd not see him again.

Katherine looked at the three bedraggled and dirty faces staring at her. If they only knew how badly she'd wanted to go, they wouldn't be so proud of her. Guilt made it very difficult to meet each of their gazes, but she had to. She looked first at Chris and Bettina, then at Kyle.

His light brown eyes watched her with a shattering intensity that took her breath away.

"I'm sorry," she began. Chris swore, and Bettina surged forward to hug her.

"It wasn't your fault," she said fiercely. "You couldn't have known your boss was psycho and insanely jealous of your career. How could you have realized he would get this desperate? Don't you dare blame yourself. Besides, his shots never came close to us."

Abruptly, Kyle stood, tugged her to her feet. Cupping her face in his hands, he said in a low, soft voice, "Are you listening to that, Katy? It's good advice."

All she could do was lick her suddenly dry lips and swallow hard. How could she explain how she felt? That because of her, innocent people had nearly died? She wanted to look away, wanted to sink into a hole and never have to face him again, but she couldn't tear her gaze away from his.

"I probably should have gone back. The press is going to need statements, and the office—"

"Can wait," he finished for her. "You nearly died," he whispered.

"And I thought you had." Her voice cracked. "I thought you had."

Bettina and Chris stood. "We'll gather the bikes," Chris offered quietly, and they walked away.

They were alone and Katherine didn't think she could handle it.

"I came back for you and saw you two tangled on the ground. Then that shot went off—" He took a deep, shuddery breath. "God, Katy. I thought you'd been taken from me."

"The bullet must have flown into the air. He passed out from the bump on his head."

"Too bad," he said darkly, with such suppressed rage, she could only stare at her mild-mannered California cowboy.

"Only two more days." *God, where had* that *come from?*

"Yes," he said seriously. "Just today and tomorrow." He moved close, that tall, rangy body just barely touching hers. "So quiet," he murmured, touching her cheek. "So perfectly in control already. Are you ever going to let go?"

Her heart hammered. "I—I don't know what you mean."

His eyes met hers. "Control is everything to you. Everything. You'd rather get it together and put on a front than show me how much you're hurting."

"I'm not hurting. I'm hardly injured."

"I'm not talking about your scratches," he said mildly, though she sensed his temper. "You were just betrayed by someone who was not only your boss, but your friend. It must hurt, Katy. It must."

It was killing her, but if she let him continue to discuss it, she would fall apart. "I'm fine."

His jaw tightened. "So when we finish this thing out, you'll just get back in your car and drive back to your world. No problem."

"That's right." Except she would miss him until her dying day.

"I have a feeling you won't easily let me fit in with you there, so where will that leave us?"

Whoever said love could conquer all was just plain wrong. Nothing could conquer her horrible, desperate feelings of guilt and overwhelming terror that she didn't deserve him. Plus, he was right. He wouldn't easily fit into her world. And all the shame that she felt over those feelings wouldn't change a thing. Still the humiliation had her turning. "We're not even off the mountain yet," she whispered. "So it's hard to tell."

For a brief, delicious fraction in time, she felt his hands lightly on her neck, her shoulders, before they were dropped away. "I guess it is," he said finally, then led her to her bike.

That night at the campfire was a quiet, solemn one. The moon had disappeared behind a patch of silvery clouds, making it dark and even more grave.

But it gave Katherine no sense of fear. The bad guy was caught. Yet a new monster threatened to overcome her.

Loneliness.

How it was possible to sit in a group of four people and feel lonely was beyond her, but she did.

Maybe it was because Chris and Bettina were typically lost in each other and that Kyle hadn't said a word.

She had one more day with him, but already he was gone from her life.

Kyle's thoughts were equally glum, but his were laced with anger, not self-pity.

How the hell can she do this? He glanced at her across the fire, staring morosely into the flames. They should be celebrating her freedom, the joy of life. Each other. Anything other than this horrible, awkward silence that he couldn't end. He couldn't, because she *had* to. She'd imposed it.

He'd told her how he felt, he'd laid his heart out on the line. Still, after all they'd been through, she refused to allow herself the victory he could taste.

She would leave tomorrow, he reminded himself. His stomach clenched because he knew, if he ever wanted to see her again, he would have to be the one to push.

He hated that.

Hated also that he knew he would. He couldn't stand the thought of losing her. In fact, if he was given one more chance, he'd throw in his trump card.

He'd tell her who he really was, if it meant he could keep her.

He'd just tell her now.

But before he could say a word, she'd mumbled her good-nights and had dived into her tent, without a backward glance.

Seems the counselor was back, and she wasn't going to give him any chance at all. Well, that was too bad, he thought with a typical and newborn thrust of optimism. He wouldn't give up. Ever. He could and would overcome this insane need she had for perfect, tight control.

He would make her see that they were meant to be, though he'd have to tread carefully. To push her would be disaster. Bullying her would be equally wrong. Tricking her would only win her distrust. No, he'd have to ease her into it, as if it were her own idea.

The fire crackled. Stars moved in their timeless pattern across the sky. Bettina and Chris snuggled close and made out.

Kyle Spencer put his thoughts together, stared into the flames, and planned.

The trek came to a beautiful, gentle, easy end eighteen hours later. They were met at the bottom of the trail by the sag wagon, Sarah and Jonathan—who wanted to hear every juicy detail—and the news-hungry press.

Kyle had watched Katy become more distant and more nervous as the day had progressed. Several times he'd stopped her and tried to get her to talk, but she'd refused.

He knew in his heart that she was preparing herself to ruthlessly end what had happened between them. It would be a typical Katherine Wilson move—destroy any iota of possible happiness before she got hurt or lost herself.

And he was powerless to stop her.

As she got off her bike and glanced toward the members of the press, he knew a spurt of real irritation with her. The counselor had taken over already, and she hadn't even taken off her helmet.

Briefly, she glanced at him again. "I guess this is it."

No. He wouldn't let it be. "Katy—"

"I'm sorry, Kyle. I've got to go. Thank you for a wonderful trip."

He could only stare at her. She was going to leave as if

nothing had ever existed between them. And he was left with the sorry choice of begging her or letting her go.

Some choice. But he'd already made his decision.

"I'll never forget it," she whispered, biting her lip and showing him the first sign of emotion he'd seen from her since the day before.

"I know you won't," he said solemnly, taking her hand and tugging her close for a hug. "Because I won't let you." He kissed her jaw, the corner of her lips, then her mouth.

She pushed away, ducking her head as he caught the glint of tears. "I have to go," she whispered, then turned.

He just managed to catch her and whip her back around. "Why, Katy?"

She could only shake her head. "It has to be this way, Kyle. I have to go."

What could he do? He wasn't about to beg her to stay, not when she was chomping at the bit to leave him, and certainly not with his crew and the press as an audience. As much as he didn't want to think about it, dealing with Katy would have to wait until after this last trip he'd planned for the summer.

Until he could give her the time and patience she needed.

For the next hour he got caught up in his good-byes with Sarah and Jonathan, then Bettina and Chris. He had to deal with his crew. His next Bonsai trip left from that very spot, in a little over three hours. The group was big—sixteen—and he was taking two other crew members. They'd be gone for fourteen days.

There wasn't a lot of time to prepare. Nor was there

the time to try to deal with Katy, though he wanted to desperately.

Keeping a watch on her from the corner of his eye, he bent to his task of checking the gear. Smoothly, efficiently, she dealt with the press. She held herself so regally, so coolly, it was hard to remember that her face was dirty, her clothes damp from her ride, and that she hadn't showered.

Disgusted, with her and himself, Kyle turned his back to her and forced his mind to focus on his chores.

Until, that is, he was grabbed from behind and tightly bear-hugged by three tall, sensual brunettes. Laughing, feeling lighthearted for the first time in too long, he turned and hugged his sisters back.

"Only three of you?" he teased, trying not to let his heart drop because he could no longer see Katy. "I thought I was taking all six, plus several husbands, a couple of no-good boyfriends, and a few girlfriends. Don't tell me some have chickened out."

"The rest of us are on our way," Sarina, his oldest sister promised, giving him another hug. "You look awful, Kyle."

He never had been able to hide a thing from his sisters, so he ducked his gaze and forced a smile. "Yeah? Well, thanks so much. You guys look pretty great." And they did. It was good to see his family again. Good to feel secure and loved. A huge lump clogged his throat.

His sister's eyes narrowed, but he shook his head, definitely not ready to talk. Immediately she backed off, but she gave him another hug. So he steeped himself in family love and told himself it would all work out.

He'd make sure of it.

❖━━━━━━━━━❖

The walk to her car, nearly a quarter of a mile, seemed short, flat, and easy. Katherine unlocked it for the first time in three weeks and slid into the seat.

It felt strange, small, and cramped. Very urban. The sound of the engine startled her. The foreign feel of the seat belt strapping her in had her squirming uncomfortably.

It would be good, she reassured herself. Good to get back into her life. Real good to face her job and the implications of all that had happened. She hadn't yet dealt with Ted's betrayal in her mind, but she would. And her job was waiting.

But it wasn't until she glanced down and saw the single wildflower poking out of her duffel bag on the passenger seat that she broke down in tears.

She couldn't do it. Who was she fooling? Kyle Spencer, her wild, free-spirited wilderness guide with an attitude, had wormed his way into her heart and soul. Yes, he was the opposite of everything she'd thought she'd ever want; carefree, easygoing, not too ambitious. But he was open, loving, sensitive, and so achingly romantic. Not to mention the most gorgeous man she'd ever met.

She was out of the car in a flash, hoofing back the quarter mile to the trail head where she'd left him, preparing for his next trip.

"So what if he only works three months out of the year," she said out loud. "He works damn hard. Obviously he makes a fine living. If he's fine with it, well, then, so am I." She kicked a branch for emphasis.

"And so what," she told a startled squirrel who raced

across her path, "if I can't control myself when I'm around him. Control is overrated anyway. Look where it got Ted." She kicked another branch, and she felt better.

Until she came through the trees, to the edge of the clearing. Kyle was kneeling on the ground, preparing an entire line of packs. A high, feminine voice called his name, and before he could look up, two long-legged, beautiful blondes jumped him.

Katherine's mouth opened and she stopped short. This is where he'd push them away, stand up, and announce his undying love for her. She waited, heart in her throat.

The women laughed and threw their arms around Kyle. One of them kissed him full on the mouth. Then another woman jumped onto the tangle of bodies and did the same thing.

Okay, Katherine thought. He'll shove them off any moment now. After all, he had just fallen in love with his last client. *Hadn't he?*

But instead of pushing anyone, Kyle laughed and hugged the woman close, rolling over on top of her and digging his fingers into her ribs until she squealed. *Squealed.* Then he gave her a smacking kiss on the cheek, swatted her bottom, and leaped to his feet.

Already they seemed to be hard-and-fast friends. Silly her for thinking what they'd had on their trek was so unique. *Seemed not to be.*

He looked at those women so . . . familiarly. So endearingly. And he looked so absolutely irresistible with his windblown hair in his eyes, his shirt snug across his broad chest, those jeans so impossibly worn and perfectly encasing the best male body she'd ever seen. Then he tugged a lock of one of the women's hair and grinned playfully.

As he'd done with her a hundred times.

She'd been tricked. Each silly, contagious grin he'd given her had made her laugh. Had made her feel special. Had made her fall a little more in love with him.

Stepping back into the trees, she clamped a hand over her mouth. She'd nearly made the mistake of a lifetime. What had she been thinking, charging through the woods, ready to proclaim her undying love?

How ridiculously mortifying it would have been if she had. He would have stared at her as if she'd lost her marbles. For to him, she was just one of a thousand clients . . . someone who trailed in and out of his life.

She was a fool.

Quietly, her heart at her feet, she went back to her car, back to her life.

Katherine sank wearily into her office chair. She'd been working like crazy the past two weeks, helping the new DA get acquainted.

Katherine had actually thought she might resign, might *need* to resign. But the new DA was a woman, and a lovely one at that. Katherine thought things would be just fine.

If only her heart didn't still ache. Every time she saw a new cloud formation, every time she walked through the park to get to work, every time she simply stopped a minute . . . the pain edged in, threatening to overcome her.

She missed Kyle more than she thought possible. For

that matter, she missed everything; being outdoors, the smell of the morning, the first drop of a quick storm. She missed it all.

But he hadn't even called her. Not once.

Sighing, she leaned back, then popped up again at the knock at her door. Her secretary came in, carrying a huge box.

"You just got this delivery," she said, setting it on her desk. She was gone again before Katherine could ask whom it had come from.

Familiar with the blue-and-white logo of the huge sporting company GO!, she stood and tried to figure out how to open the box.

Who would have sent her something?

Finally, she tore the thing open with her letter opener and separated the tissue paper. The minute her eyes settled on the brand-new backpack, her heart started to pound. The note attached directed her to the inside pocket.

Inside, she found a Bonsai Trails ticket pouch, holding a ticket for one for a Bonsai adventure starting . . . to-morrow!

Bring the backpack, the last line said. *You'll need it.*

Joy filled her heart while tears filled her eyes. He'd contacted her. He'd sent her a ticket for a new trek. Had he read her mind? Grabbing her purse, buttoning her jacket, she wrote a note to her new boss, explaining she needed a quick leave of absence.

This was her dream job, the one she'd wanted and sought for years. But now she didn't even care if she lost it.

She was going on this adventure and she was going to

make Kyle love her. No more bitchy attorney. No more stubborn aloofness.

She wanted him and she'd prove it.

Nervous, full of expectation and suppressed hope, Katherine prepared herself the next morning.

It was just an invitation for a trip, she reminded herself brutally. Not an invitation to spend forever.

But hadn't he once said that very thing was his greatest wish? Had he been playing her? Joking with her?

God, she hoped not.

This time their meeting place was right in town. She expected a bus stop or a park. Somewhere they'd all be shuttled to the trail head.

She didn't expect to drive up to the sleek, bold downtown corporate headquarters of GO! Carefully, she checked the address on the tickets, then knew a moment of dread.

Was this all a joke?

Still, she got out of her car and took the backpack. For the first time she noticed that the address said twenty-sixth floor. The penthouse?

The elevator was so fast, her head spun. Or was that her nerves?

She was hopelessly out of place in this fancy office interior in her jeans, boots, and T-shirt, and accepted more than her fair share of strange and appreciative looks.

Then she realized just a few weeks earlier she wouldn't have been caught dead out in public so casually dressed. But it felt right.

A young woman wearing a beautiful but conservative blue suit passed her, her lips tightening in disapproval. It should have humiliated Katherine, would have in the not-too-distant past.

Not now. Not when she was fairly certain she was the most comfortably dressed person in the building.

Heart tripping, stomach unsettled, she made her way down the hall and faced the beautiful, elegant reception-ist. She swallowed hard and stumbled over her words as she realized she had no idea exactly what she was doing there.

But the woman took one look at her and smiled a friendly, open smile. "Ms. Wilson?"

Numbly, Katherine nodded.

"This way," the woman said, and led her directly to the corner office.

What the hell was going on? Feeling as though she'd entered the Twilight Zone, she followed. The next thing she knew, the secretary had announced her, gently pushed her into the office, and shut the door behind her.

A man stood at the windows, his broad, tapered back to her, his hands in his trouser pockets. Even from her distance, she could see his expensive suit, how coolly ele-gant he held himself. He was definitely used to such luxu-rious surroundings, and such magnificent attire.

And he was Kyle.

FIFTEEN

"Kyle?" Katherine gasped. "What—"

He turned to face her and she had to gasp again. She'd never seen him look like this, so amazingly polished, re-fined . . . *affluent*.

"Hello, Katy." The voice was the same—silky, low, husky. Sexy. But his trademark crooked smile was missing. So was the light in his eyes.

"I don't get it," she whispered, holding up the backpack. "Why are you dressed like that?" Never having seen him in anything but jeans, it was a bit bewildering to see him dressed to the nines and looking so comfortable. Not to mention so devastatingly handsome. "I thought this was about another trip."

"It is." He licked his lips, and she realized he was as nervous as she was. "It's about the trip of a lifetime. Did you look inside the pack, Katy?"

She nodded. "It's empty."

"Check the inside pocket."

Fingers fumbling, she slid her hand into the pocket.

Her fingers froze on a small velvet box. Slowly she pulled it out. A jewelry box. No, a *ring box*. Shaking, she dropped it twice.

On the second time Kyle smiled soberly and stooped down next to where she knelt on the floor, staring at it. Scooping it up, he looked at her. "Aren't you going to open it?"

She couldn't take her eyes off the black velvet box in his hand. Her blood roared in her ears. "I don't think I can," she said, her voice quivering. "I'm shaking."

Gently, he reached for her hand while his other popped open the box. He then set the opened box in her hand.

She stared down at the beautiful diamond ring. "Oh, Kyle."

"I love you," he said huskily. "I don't want this to be over." Now he reached for her other hand and met her startled gaze. "Yes, you have your world, and I have mine—"

"Yours doesn't seem to be what I thought it was," she said, looking around at their luxurious office surroundings with confusion.

He smiled, a little self-deprecatory. "No. And I'm sorry for that. But God, Katy. This first. Please, this first." He squeezed her hand, then tipped her face up to his. Between them, their joined hands held the ring. "You're holding my ring."

"Yes," she whispered, and bit her lip. "But there's so much—"

"No." He shook his head, his heart in his throat. "Nothing matters but this." Nothing had ever mattered more. "Love *does* conquer all, Katy. We can have it all, if you're only willing to try. Please, say you'll marry me."

Her eyes filled. "I thought you didn't want me anymore, that I'd been just a diversion. You didn't call—"

"I couldn't," he whispered back, aching at the pain he'd caused, even as his heart soared with hope. "I was on that trip, and this had to be done in person."

"I came back to see you that day." Now her voice was tough, accusing, and his gut tightened. "I wanted to throw myself at you and beg you to keep me. You were with your new group. Already laughing and hugging like you were old friends."

Now he understood, and he laughed with relief.

She let go of the ring and punched his shoulder. "I thought you were just playing with me, all that talk of forever and . . ."

"Love?" he asked gently, tenderness filling him. He grabbed her resisting body close and kissed her hard. "I was laughing and hugging those women," he admitted, tightening his grip when she would have yanked away, "because we *were* old friends. They're my sisters."

It took a moment to sink in, but when it did, she moaned with embarrassment. "Your sisters."

"That's right." He gave her a wicked smile as happiness overcame him. "Now tell me," he said, moving in close to taste her neck. "What was that about throwing yourself at me?"

When he opened his mouth on her throat, she fisted her hands in his suit jacket and held him close. Then she stilled. "As soon as you tell me why you're dressed this way. And looking as if you were born with a silver spoon in your mouth."

"Oh, that."

"Yeah. *That*." Now her hands were on her hips, those gray eyes filled with suspicion. "It just occurred to me. Didn't GO! used to be called Spencer's Great Outdoors?"

Snagging her hips, he tried to pull her close again, but she was having none of it. He sighed and fingered the ring box. "Still is," he muttered. "Sometimes."

"Kyle *Spencer*," she said, then closed her eyes and shook her head. "I'm an idiot."

"No—"

"Be quiet, Mr. Spencer," she admonished, turning from him. "I have to think a minute."

"But—"

"You lied to me."

"No, I—"

"You let me think you were something you weren't."

"Now wait a minute," he said, turning her around. "I never did that. I am who you saw out there on the mountain, Katy. No one else. Never anyone else. That's why I didn't tell you. I had to make sure you liked that person." He stroked her cheek. "It was very important to me that you did."

"Why did you think I wouldn't? Because I was a snob?"

"Yeah." He smiled and kissed her softly. "But you got over that, didn't you? Tell me you did."

"You know I did." She sighed and wrapped her arms around him. "All that time I wasted wanting you to be something else. Then it didn't matter anymore. I loved you for exactly who you were. Now—"

"Wait," he said hoarsely, his hands digging into her waist. "What did you just say?"

"All that time—"

"No," he cut her off with a growl. "After that."

"That it didn't matter—"

"Dammit, Katy."

She laughed and hugged him. "I love you, Kyle Spencer, mountainman and entrepreneur. I'm not used to these things, but I'm pretty sure it's for now and forever."

He realized how new this was for her, how difficult. But he had to be positive. "Pretty sure?"

She nodded.

"What can I do to fully convince you?"

She bit her lip and laughed a little. Still unsure. "You could give me all the words that I've waited so long to hear from you. You could kiss me and tell me again you love me. That you want me forever. That without me your life is nothing."

Now he smiled, slow and wide. "I can do that," he whispered, opening the box and slipping the ring on her finger. Then he gathered her close and gave her what he'd promised.

EPILOGUE

She waited, but it was difficult. After all, it took them nearly a week to hike in as far as she needed them to.

"What is this about, Legs?" Kyle demanded from right behind her. "We have to hurry or we'll get caught in the storm that's following us."

Katherine glanced up, caught sight of the gray, wispy clouds to the north that indicated autumn had long past arrived and winter was on its way. "So we'll hide out in the tent until it passes."

He groaned. "I have to be back at the office, I told you that. I have a meeting—"

"Meeting, schmeeting," she chanted, then laughed. "Do you realize how ironic this is? You're worried about your job and I could care less about mine?"

"Easy for you to say," he grumbled, stepping over the heavy fall foliage. "You don't have a job. Not since you so gleefully quit last month."

"That's right." She laughed again, feeling so light she could fly. "Now I don't have a real job until the summer.

Thanks for agreeing to let me be your assistant this year," she added politely.

He growled again, caught up with her, and whipped her around. "You're not my assistant," he said carefully, enunciating each word through his teeth. "You're my mate. My lover. You're going to be my wife, if I could just get you to hold still long enough to get to a justice of the peace."

"I want a real wedding. You promised. In December."

"December is too far away."

"Only two months." Ah, they were here. The spot she'd been searching for these last few days. With a wicked gleam in her eyes, she backed him to the tree. *Their tree.*

"What are you doing?" But he smiled as she pressed her body to his, suggestively rubbing her hips over his own. "Temptress. We have to get off this ridge before dark and back down into that meadow or—" His words broke off on a moan as her caresses got bolder.

"I wanted to bring you here," she whispered, breathless from what she was doing to him. "I know it took all week and that this is a bad time. But we had to be here when I told you."

"Told me what?"

She held him still when he would have straightened away from the tree. "Kyle, I love you."

He smiled, a sweet, beautiful smile that never failed to turn her heart upside down. "I know that." He lifted her hands and kissed the sores on her palms that were still healing from that fateful day when she'd had her run-in with Ted.

"And you love me," she pointed out, her breath quickening over his gentle touch.

Another grin. "I knew there was a brain in that lovely head of yours, sweetheart."

To silence him, she kissed him until they were both panting. Then she lifted her head and stared up into the face she loved beyond reason. "We've been here before."

"Yeah," he whispered, snagging her hips in his big hands and rocking them to his. "Look what remembering is doing to me."

He was hard. And huge. He was hers. "Well," she said with a little nervous laugh. "We're going to have a reminder of that day for a very long time to come."

"I've got your reminder right here." And he rubbed that "reminder" over her again.

Her eyes closed, her breath clogged her throat. "Kyle," she said in an unnaturally high voice. "I'm trying to tell you something. Something important."

He went still. "Okay."

"Did I tell you I love you?" God, she was nervous. Yes, they planned to be married. Yes, she knew he loved her, as ridiculously as she loved him, thank God. But she wasn't sure how he would feel about the rest.

"You've told me," he said, still not moving a muscle. "And while I love hearing that, why do I have the feeling I'd rather hear your news?"

She ran her fingers over his wide, hard shoulders, down his back. She grasped his waist and hugged tightly. Then, with a sigh, she took a step back. "There's so much we haven't discussed," she said earnestly. "Like what your favorite color is. Where we'll explore next summer. If you like homemade meat loaf."

He let out a little, frustrated laugh. "Blue. Montana. Yes, very much, though I didn't know you could cook."

"Of course I can. I can—"

His strong arms surrounded her, banded her close, silencing her. His eyes met hers. *"Tell me."*

Unsettled, she took a deep breath. Her hands slipped down his body to her own flat tummy. "You know, I've grown kinda attached to this tree," she whispered. She licked her lips. "Do you think we could come visit it every year? Sort of as a tradition?"

His gaze dropped to her hands, which protectively held her stomach. Eyes sparkling with bare emotion, he lifted his gaze back to hers. *"Why?"* His own voice was soft and so low she could hardly hear him.

"It was here, in these woods, that it began."

Now those light brown eyes she loved were filled with a desperate need for the truth. "God, Katy, just tell me."

"I'm pregnant."

He blinked, and moisture appeared in his incredibly expressive eyes. "A baby," he whispered, and covered her hands with his own. "Oh, Katy, I'd hoped so." Holding her stomach, he kissed her, deeply, and the slow healing of her last wound began.

THE EDITORS' CORNER

Everybody has a classic story that has endured in their heart through the years. There's always that one story that makes you think *What if . . . ?* This month we present four new LOVESWEPTs, each based on a treasured tale of the past, with their own little twists of fate. It is said that differences keep people apart, but we've found the opposite to be true. Differences make life interesting, adding zest and spice to our lives. We hope you'll enjoy exploring those differences in opinion, station, and attitude that ensure a happy ending for our LOVESWEPT characters this month.

In Pat Van Wie's **ROUGH AROUND THE EDGES,** LOVESWEPT #870, Kristen Helton is about to meet her match in one doozy of a hero, Alex Jamison. Alex grew up on the streets of Miami and now he's devoted his life to keeping the local community center open. But when Kristen insists on joining his fight to keep kids out of trouble, Alex has to accept that he may have been wrong about the gorgeous young doctor. The tensions run high after Alex decides to sacrifice himself to raise money for the center. Kristen discovers his secret and comes to realize that maybe their worlds aren't so different after all. In the true tradition of Robin Hood, Pat Van Wie delights as she shows us how we must persevere against all odds.

Maureen Caudill is giving Jason Cooper his comeuppance in **NEVER SAY GOOD-BYE,** LOVESWEPT #871. When last seen, Jason was playing the part of die-hard bachelor scoffing at his sister and best friend's domestic bliss in DADDY CANDIDATE, LOVESWEPT #797. Years later, C. J. Stone's magazine names Jason the Sexiest Businessman in California. Now Jason is desperate to get C.J. off his back and believes that a nerdy facade will make her change her mind about him. C.J. and Jason seem to disagree about everything. Even watching *It's a Wonderful Life* causes a clash of beliefs between them. But the one thing they can't argue about is their growing attraction to each other—it's undeniable. With humor and grace, Maureen Caudill plots a collision course for these mismatched lovers.

Stephanie Bancroft retells the story of Aladdin in **YOUR WISH IS MY COMMAND,** LOVESWEPT #872. "I shall grant you three of your heart's desires" is the last thing Ladden Sanderson expects to hear after an earthquake reduces his antiques store to a shambles. Jasmine Crowne doesn't understand why now, after three years of friendship, she suddenly longs to feel Ladden's arms around her. And no one can explain the strange man who keeps muttering something about wishes—or the antique carpet Ladden is reserving for Jasmine that keeps popping up in the weirdest places. Can a benevolent genie help this quiet diamond in the rough win over the woman he's always loved? Stephanie Bancroft charms readers as she weaves a delectable romance liberally spiced with marvelous miracles and fantasy.

Five years ago Liam Bartlett was saved from a San Salustiano prison with the help of young freedom fighter Marisala Bolivar. Now Mara is all grown up and both are about to learn **FREEDOM'S PRICE**, LOVESWEPT #873, by Suzanne Brockmann. When Mara's uncle sends her to Boston to get an education and, unbeknownst to her, learn to be a proper lady, he asks his friend Liam to take care of her, to be her guardian. Liam finds it harder and harder to see Mara as the young girl she once was, but his promise to her uncle stands in his way. Mara has loved Liam forever, and she does her best to get him to see her as the woman she has become. Suzanne Brockmann seals the fate of two lovers as they learn to battle the past and look to the future.

Happy reading!

With warmest wishes,

Susann Brailey

Joy abella

Susann Brailey
Senior Editor

Joy Abella
Administrative Editor

P.S. Watch for these Bantam women's fiction titles coming in January! Hailed as "an accomplished story-teller" by the *Los Angeles Daily News*, nationally best-selling author Jane Feather concludes her charm bracelet trilogy with **THE EMERALD SWAN.** An exquisite emerald charm sets in motion a tale of suspense, laughter, and love, and brings together twin girls separated on a night of terror. Newcomer Shana Abé delivers **A ROSE IN WINTER.** In the year 1280, a time of dark turbulence, Solange is forced to scorn her greatest love in order to protect him, an act that leaves her imprisoned in the terrifying reaches of hell until Damon becomes her unwitting rescuer. From *New York Times* bestselling author Iris Johansen comes a new hardcover novel of suspense, **AND THEN YOU DIE. . . .** Photojournalist Bess Grady witnesses a nightmarish experiment conducted by international conspirators. With the help of a mysterious agent, Bess escapes their clutches, vowing to do whatever it takes to stop them from succeeding in their deadly plan. And immediately following this page, preview the Bantam women's fiction titles on sale in December!

For current information on Bantam's women's fiction, visit our new Web site, *Isn't It Romantic,* at the following address:
http://www.bdd.com/romance

"A dark, powerful tale of nerve-shattering suspense." —Tami Hoag

THE PERFECT HUSBAND

by Lisa Gardner

Jim Beckett was everything she'd ever dreamed of. But two years after Tess married the decorated cop and bore his child, she helped put him behind bars for savagely murdering ten women. Even locked up in a maximum security prison, he vowed he would come after her and make her pay. Now the cunning killer has escaped—and the most dangerous game of all begins. . . .

After a lifetime of fear, Tess will do something she's never done before. She's going to learn to protect her daughter and fight back, with the help of a burned-out ex-marine. As the largest manhunt four states have ever seen mobilizes to catch Beckett, the clock winds down to the terrifying reunion between husband and wife. And Tess knows that this time, her only choices are to kill—or be killed.

Tess Williams awoke as she'd learned to awaken— slowly, degree by degree, so that she reached consciousness without ever giving herself away. First her ears woke up, seeking out the sound of another person breathing. Next, her skin prickled to life, searching for the burning length of her husband's body pressed against her back. Finally, when her ears registered no sound and her skin found her alone in her bed, her eyes opened, going automatically to the closet and checking the small wooden chair she'd jammed beneath the doorknob in the middle of the night.

The chair was still in place. She released the breath she'd been holding and sat up. The empty room was already bright with mid-morning sun, the adobe walls golden and cheery. The air was hot. Her T-shirt stuck to her back, but maybe the sweat came from nightmares that never quite went away. She'd once liked mornings. They were difficult for her now, but not as difficult as night, when she would lie there and try to force her eyes to give up their vigilant search of shadows in favor of sleep.

You made it, she told herself. *You actually made it.*

For the last two years she'd been running, clutching her four-year-old daughter's hand and trying to convince Samantha that everything would be all right. She'd picked up aliases like decorative accessories and new addresses like spare parts. But she'd never really escaped. Late at night, she would sit at the edge of her daughter's bed, stroking Samantha's golden hair, and stare at the closet with fatalistic eyes.

She knew just what kind of monsters hid in the closet. She had seen the crime scene photos of what they could do. Three weeks ago, her personal monster had broken out of a maximum security prison by beating two guards to death in under sixty seconds.

Tess had called Lieutenant Lance Difford. He'd called Vince. The wheels were set in motion. Tess Williams had hidden Samantha safely away, then she had traveled as far as she could travel. Then she had traveled some more.

First, she'd taken the train, and the train had taken her through New England fields of waving grass and industrial sectors of twisted metal. Then she'd caught a plane, flying over everything as if that would help her forget and covering so many miles she left behind even fall and returned to summer.

Landing in Phoenix was like arriving in a moon crater: everything was red, dusty, and bordered by distant blue mountains. She'd never seen palms; here roads were lined with them. She'd never seen cactus; here they covered the land like an encroaching army.

The bus had only moved her farther into alien terrain. The red hills had disappeared, the sun had gained fury. Signs for cities had been replaced by signs reading STATE PRISON IN AREA. DO NOT STOP FOR HITCHHIKERS.

The reds and browns had seeped away until the bus rolled through sun-baked amber and bleached-out greens. The mountains no longer followed like kindly grandfathers. In this strange, harsh land of southern Arizona, even the hills were tormented, flayed alive methodically by mining trucks and bull-dozers.

It was the kind of land where you really did expect to turn and see the OK Corral. The kind of land where lizards were beautiful and coyotes cute. The kind of land where the hothouse rose died and the prickly cactus lived.

It was perfect.

Tess climbed out of bed. She moved slowly. Her right leg was stiff and achy, the jagged scar twitching with ghost pains. Her left wrist throbbed, ringed by a harsh circle of purple bruises. She could tell it wasn't anything serious—her father had taught her a lot about broken bones. As things went in her life these days, a bruised wrist was the least of her concerns.

She turned her attention to the bed.

She made it without thinking, tucking the corners

tightly and smoothing the covers with military precision.

I want to be able to bounce a quarter off that bed, Theresa. Youth is no excuse for sloppiness. You must always seek to improve.

She caught herself folding back the edge of the sheet over the light blanket and dug her fingertips into her palms. In a deliberate motion, she ripped off the blanket and dumped it on the floor.

"I will not make the bed this morning," she stated to the empty room. "I choose not to make the bed."

She wouldn't clean anymore either, or wash dishes or scrub floors. She remembered too well the scent of ammonia as she rubbed down the windows, the doorknobs, the banisters. She'd found the pungent odor friendly, a deep-clean sort of scent.

This is my house, and not only does it look clean, but it smells clean.

Later, Lieutenant Difford had explained to her how ammonia was one of the few substances that rid surfaces of fingerprints.

Now she couldn't smell ammonia without feeling ill.

Her gaze was drawn back to the bed, the rumpled sheets, the covers tossed and wilted on the floor. For a moment, the impulse, the sheer *need* to make that bed—and make it right because she had to seek to improve herself, you should always seek to improve— nearly overwhelmed her. Sweat beaded her upper lip. She fisted her hands to keep them from picking up the blankets.

"Don't give in. He messed with your mind, Tess, but that's done now. You belong to yourself and you are tough. You won, dammit. You *won*."

The words didn't soothe her. She crossed to the

bureau to retrieve her gun from her purse. Only at the last minute did she remember that the .22 had fallen on the patio.

J.T. Dillon had it now.

She froze. She had to have her gun. She ate with her gun, slept with her gun, walked with her gun. She couldn't be weaponless. *Defenseless, vulnerable, weak.*

Oh God. Her breathing accelerated, her stomach plummeted, and her head began to spin. She walked the edge of the anxiety attack, feeling the shakes and knowing that she either found solid footing now or lunged into the abyss.

Breathe, Tess, breathe. But the friendly desert air kept flirting with her lungs. She bent down and forcefully caught a gulp by her knees, squeezing her eyes shut.

"Can I walk you home?"

She was startled. "You mean me?" She hugged her school books more tightly against her Mt. Greylock High sweater. She couldn't believe the police officer was addressing her. She was not the sort of girl handsome young men addressed.

"No," he teased lightly. "I'm talking to the grass." He pushed himself away from the tree, his smile unfurling to reveal two charming dimples. All the girls in her class talked of those dimples, dreamed of those dimples. "You're Theresa Matthews, right?"

She nodded stupidly. She should move. She knew she should move. She was already running late for the store and her father did not tolerate tardiness.

She remained standing there, staring at this young man's handsome face. He looked so strong. A man of the law. A man of integrity? For one moment she found herself thinking, If I told you everything, would you save me? Would somebody please save me?

"*Well, Theresa Matthews, I'm Officer Beckett. Jim Beckett.*"

"*I know.*" *Her gaze fell to the grass.* "*Everyone knows who you are.*"

"*May I walk you home, Theresa Matthews? Would you allow me the privilege?*"

She remained uncertain, too overwhelmed to speak. Her father would kill her. Only promiscuous young women, evil women, enticed men to walk them home. But she didn't want to send Jim Beckett away. She didn't know what to do.

He leaned over and winked at her. His blue eyes were so clear, so calm. So steady.

"*Come on, Theresa, I'm a cop. If you can't trust me, who can you trust?*"

"I won," she muttered by her knees. "Dammit, I won!"

But she wanted to cry. She'd won, but the victory remained hollow, the price too high. He'd done things to her that never should have been done. He'd taken things from her that she couldn't afford to lose. Even now, he was still in her head.

Someday soon, he would kill her. He'd promised to cut out her still-beating heart, and Jim always did what he said.

She forced her head up. She took a deep breath. She pressed her fists against her thighs. "Fight, Tess. It's all you have left."

She pushed away from the dresser and moved to her suitcase, politely brought to her room by Freddie. She'd made it here, step one of her plan. Next, she had to get J.T. to agree to train her. Dimly, she remembered mentioning her daughter to him. That had been a mistake. Never tell them more than you have to, never tell the truth if a lie will suffice.

Maybe J.T. wouldn't remember. He hadn't seemed too sober. Vincent should've warned her about his drinking.

She didn't know much about J.T. Vince had said J.T. was the kind of man who could do anything he wanted to, but who didn't seem to want to do much. He'd been raised in a wealthy, well-connected family in Virginia, attended West Point, but then left for reasons unknown and joined the Marines. Then he'd left the Marines and struck out solo, rapidly earning a reputation for a fearlessness bordering on insanity. As a mercenary, he'd drifted toward doing the impossible and been indifferent to anything less. He hated politics, loved women. He was fanatical about fulfilling his word and noncommittal about everything else.

Five years ago, he'd up and left the mercenary business without explanation. Like the prodigal son, he'd returned to Virginia and in a sudden flurry of unfathomable activity, he'd married, adopted a child, and settled down in the suburbs as if all along he'd really been a shoe salesman. Later, a sixteen-year-old with a new Camaro and even newer license had killed J.T.'s wife and son in a head-on collision.

And J.T. had disappeared in Arizona.

She hadn't expected him to be drinking. She hadn't expected him to still appear so strong. She'd pictured him as being older, maybe soft and overripe around the middle, a man who'd once been in his prime but now was melting around the edges. Instead, he'd smelled of tequila. His body had been toned and hard. He'd moved fast, pinning her without any effort. He had black hair, covering his head, his arms, his chest.

Jim had had no hair, not on his head, not on his body. He'd been completely hairless, smooth as marble. Like a swimmer, she'd thought, and only later understood the full depth of her naiveté. Jim's touch had always been cold and dry, as if he was too perfect for such things as sweat. The first time she'd heard him urinate, she'd felt a vague sense of surprise; he gave the impression of being above such basic biological functions.

Jim had been perfect. Mannequin perfect. If only she'd held that thought longer.

She'd stick with J.T. Dillon. He'd once saved orphans. He'd been married and had a child. He'd destroyed things for money. He sounded skilled, he appeared dangerous.

For her purposes, he would do.

And if helping her cost J.T. Dillon too much?

She already knew the answer, she'd spent years coming to terms with it.

Sometimes, she did wish she was sixteen again. She'd been a normal girl, once. She'd dreamed of a white knight who would rescue her. Someone who would never hit her. Someone who would hold her close and tell her she was finally safe.

Now, she remembered the feel of her finger tightening around the trigger. The pull of the trigger, the jerk of the trigger, the roar of the gun and the ringing in her ears.

The acrid smell of gunpowder and the hoarse sound of Jim's cry. The thud of his body falling down. The raw scent of fresh blood pooling on her carpet.

She remembered these things.

And she knew she could do anything.

From award-winning author Patricia Potter comes a spectacular novel set in the wild Scottish Highlands, where a daring beauty and a fearless lord defy treachery and danger to find their heart's destiny . . .

STARCATCHER
by Patricia Potter

Marsali Gunn had been betrothed to Patrick Sutherland when she was just a girl, yet even then she knew the handsome warrior would have no rival in her heart or her dreams. But when Patrick returns from distant battlefields, a bitter feud has shattered the alliance between clans, and Marsali prepares to wed another chieftain. Boldly, Patrick steals what is rightfully his, damning the consequences. And Marsali is forced to make a choice: between loyalty to her people or a still-burning love that could plunge her and Patrick into the center of a deadly war . . .

"Patricia Potter has a special gift for giving an audience a first-class romantic story line."
—*Affaire de Coeur*

"One of the romance genre's finest talents."
—*Romantic Times*

He had dreamed of her. It was so much more than she'd ever expected. Her legs trembled as his tongue touched her lips, then slipped inside her mouth. A wave of new sensations rushed through her. Yet she did nothing to discourage the intimate way he explored her. Instead, she found herself responding to his every touch.

Somehow, with what was left of her wits, she realized she was clinging to him, as if her life were forfeit. She heard the small, throaty sounds she was making. She felt his entire body shaking, and she felt the hard, vital evidence of his manhood pressed against her. She had heard servants talk; she knew where this was leading. And she wanted it, wanted to move even closer to him, to join her body intimately with his.

But she could not build her own happiness on the blood of others, especially not the blood of her kin and the kin of the man she loved.

She had to return to Abernie. She had to go through with the wedding. . . .

Tearing herself from Patrick's embrace, Marsali let out a pained, hopeless cry. Surprised, Patrick let her go, his arms dropping to his sides. His breathing was ragged as his eyes questioned her.

"I canna," she said brokenly.

"We were pledged," he replied, his voice hoarse. "You are mine, Marsali."

The note of possessiveness in his voice, even given the feelings he aroused in her, stunned her. The flat, almost emotionless tone was so authoritative, so . . . certain. He'd become a stranger again, one who made decisions without consulting her.

"Our betrothal was broken," she said quietly, "cried off by both families."

"Not by me," he said.

She studied him obliquely. "My father and Edward . . . they will go after your family," she said.

"They will *try*." Coldness underlined his voice.

"Your father killed my aunt," she said desperately.

"Nay, my father is as puzzled by her disappearance as any man, and, despite his faults, he does not lie."

"Not even with death as a consequence?"

"Not even then."

Lifting her chin a notch, Marsali continued. "He accused my aunt of adultery."

"He says there was proof," Patrick replied.

His eyes glittered with the hardness of stone, and she glimpsed what his enemies must have seen of Patrick Sutherland. The thought of him at war with her father and brother made her shiver.

Dear Mother in heaven. The wedding should have started by now. Everyone would be looking for the bride. When would they begin to suspect the Sutherlands?

"I have to return to Abernie," she whispered.

"Jeanie said she would not help us if she wasn't sure you didna want the wedding," Patrick said flatly. "Was she wrong, lass? Do you want to wed Sinclair?"

"Aye," Marsali said defiantly, even though she was certain the lie must be plain on her face.

"Because of your sister?" Patrick guessed.

"Because you and I can never be."

He studied her for a moment, then, slowly, the tension left his face. He lifted his hand to trail a finger along her cheek. "You have become a beautiful woman," he said quietly. "But then, I always knew you would."

Her resolve melted under the words, under the intensity of his gaze, under the force of his demand for the truth. She leaned into his touch, craving it.

His hands were strong, she thought, from years of wielding a sword. But she could well destroy him, as well as both of their families, if she did not return.

"I *agreed* to the marriage with Edward," she said as firmly as she could. "I gave him my troth."

His hand trailed downward over her shoulder, her arm, until he took her hand in his. He squeezed her fingers, saying, "You had already given it to me with your words and, a minute ago, you gave it to me with your body. Your heart is mine, Marsali."

"And *your* heart?" she asked.

A muscle flexed in his throat, but he said nothing, and she wondered for a moment whether he had come for her out of affection—or simply because she was a belonging he wasn't ready to forfeit.

She pulled away and turned to gaze at the rocks, the hills, anything but the face made even more attractive to her by the character the years had given it. "Where would we go?"

"To Brinaire," he said flatly.

"And Cecilia?"

"Aye, she will come with us. You will both be safe there."

"Your father? He agrees?"

He hesitated long enough that she knew the answer.

"He will have to," he said. "Or we will go to France. I have friends there."

She turned and looked at him again. "And then our clans will fight one another. Many will die or starve because of us. Can you live with that?"

His mouth twisted. "They seem destined to fight now in any event."

"But there has been naught but a few minor raids," she said. "If I were to go with you, my father would not be satisfied with anything but blood. His pride—"

"Damn his pride!" Patrick burst out. "I canna

stand aside and see you marry Sinclair. The man is a coward. And his wife's death was more than a little odd."

When she only stared at him, saying nothing, he sighed heavily and shoved his fingers through his thick, black hair. Her gaze followed the gesture, falling on the scar on his wrist that he'd gotten saving her ferret's life so many years ago. Reaching out, she took Patrick's hand in hers, her fingers touching the rough, white mark from the hawk's talons. Its jagged length ran from the first knuckle of his fourth finger down his forearm to four inches past his wrist.

"Will you make an oath to me, Patrick Sutherland?" she asked, lifting her gaze to meet his.

"Aye," he said, nodding slowly. "Anything but return you to Sinclair."

"Send my sister away. Send her someplace safe. I know only my father's friends."

His gaze bore into hers. "I do know someone. Rufus's family. I was wounded, and they cared for me. There are five sisters, as well as Rufus and an older brother and his wife. It is as fine a family as I've ever known—and as generous a one. They live in an old keep in the Lowlands and socialize very little, though they bear a fine name. Their clan is very loyal to them."

"Will you see her safely there? Do you swear? No matter what happens between you and me?" She heard the desperation in her voice and saw, by the fierce glitter in his eyes, that he'd heard it, too.

"I swear it, lass," he said.

"Thank you." Marsali closed her eyes briefly.

She didn't resist when he took her in his arms again, pulling her gently toward him. She leaned against him, listening to the beating of his heart, the fine strong rhythm of it, and savoring the warmth of his body.

For a long minute, she huddled within his embrace, trying not to think of Abernie Castle, trying not to imagine the worry everyone—everyone but Jeanie—must be feeling by now. Shortly, when a search of the castle didn't turn up either her or Cecilia, panic would seize them. The two daughters of the keep gone without a trace.

She had to return. Still, she would not be returning the same person as she was when she left. Fear had turned into hope, if not happiness. Patrick had given her the means to refuse the marriage to Edward Sinclair. As long as she knew Cecilia was safe, no one would be able to force the words from her mouth. And by refusing marriage with Sinclair, she would break the alliance that would have crushed Patrick's family. Her father could not attack the Sutherlands on his own. Perhaps a war could be prevented, after all.

She would make her father believe that no Sutherland was involved in her sister's disappearance. Only herself. He would be furious. But he could do little.

Her heart would never be whole again. She could already feel it breaking, shattering into tiny shards of pain. But she would have the comfort of knowing she had prevented bloodshed.

She only wished that, one day, her father—and brother—might understand what she had given up.

On sale in January:

*AND THEN
YOU DIE . . .*
by Iris Johansen

*THE EMERALD
SWAN*
by Jane Feather

*A ROSE
IN WINTER*
by Shana Abé